Lashed But Not Leashed

By Mark McShane

LASHED BUT NOT LEASHED
THE STRAIGHT AND CROOKED
THE PASSING OF EVIL
SEANCE ON A WET AFTERNOON
UNTIMELY RIPPED
THE GIRL NOBODY KNOWS
NIGHT'S EVIL
THE WAY TO NOWHERE
THE CRIMSON MADNESS OF LITTLE DOOM
ILL MET BY A FISH SHOP ON GEORGE STREET
THE MAN WHO LEFT WELL ENOUGH
THE SINGULAR CASE OF THE MULTIPLE DEAD
THE HEADLESS SNOWMAN
SEANCE FOR TWO
THE OTHELLO COMPLEX

Lashed But Not Leashed

MARK McSHANE

PUBLISHED FOR THE CRIME CLUB BY
DOUBLEDAY & COMPANY, INC.
GARDEN CITY, NEW YORK
1976

All of the characters in this book are fictitious, and any resemblance to actual persons, living or dead, is purely coincidental.

Library of Congress Cataloging in Publication Data

McShane, Mark, 1930–
Lashed but not leashed.

I. Title.
PZ4.M176Las3 [PR6063.A278] 823'.9'14
ISBN 0-385-12154-7
Library of Congress Catalog Card Number 76-2801

Copyright © 1976 by Mark McShane
All Rights Reserved
Printed in the United States of America
First Edition

Lashed But Not Leashed

ONE

"Fifi!"

The small black poodle frisked on, regardless. Having the appearance of a lamb, its abandon suggested preparation for adult waywardness.

Jeremy Wood was jealous. Sternly, pouting his stomach, he called to his dog again. For the second time he was ignored. Drawing in air for a third call, Jeremy Wood paused and looked quickly all around.

It occurred to him, with a twinge of dismay in his groin, that he might have a watcher, a listener. Walking a toy poodle was bad enough, he thought, faintly cringing; but shouting "Fifi" all over the place—that was too much.

Then he saw safety. This section of Hampstead Heath had no other strollers.

However: Jeremy deepened his voice to snap, "Come here, dog." You never knew.

Fifi scampered on, heading toward a copse. Shrugging on the outside while inside taking a grim satisfaction from his defeat as master, Jeremy followed. He swung the leash and thought:

It's all Alice's fault. Bloody Alice.

A mild-looking man, Jeremy Wood, like an absconder. His carriage was hesitant, springless. He dressed neatly. Under average height, he was as thin and pale as workhouse soup.

Jeremy's manner hinted at an eagerness to please, even if it involved a diminishing of self. His true ethos home lay in that upper, sophisticated level of masochism, tyranny.

For the adjective in his thought "Bloody Alice," Jeremy felt guilty. It was a bit strong. He now changed it to "Flipping Alice."

Jeremy Wood was thirty-six years old. He looked younger. His round, pale face was unlined by time and strife. He had large dark eyes, a pointed chin, and a small nose and mouth. His hair, faded mouse-brown, fell into a wave over one ear. He came close to being elfin, which in despondent moments he suspected.

It was a face that cried out for a beard, a scowl, a scar; a face you would like at once and forget faster.

Jeremy wondered just who Alice thought she was anyway.

This summer evening, Jeremy wore flannels, tweed jacket, checked shirt, and plain green tie. It was his habitual mufti, into which he hustled on returning from his shop, Wood's Rustic Furniture, where he wore corduroys, Wellington boots, and a bucolic sweater. He hated that outfit, but was convinced that it helped.

All Jeremy's clothes were bought by Alice. She had done so for the ten years of their marriage. The sole fracture to this had been recently, a month ago, when Jeremy, in a show of muffled authority, had gone alone to get a new pair of shoes.

He picked them out of the window and tried them on. The salesman said an erudite, "Too big, sir," so Jeremy, still in authority's grip, said briskly, "Not at all." He wanted to add something devastating, but couldn't think what. Again he said, "Not at all." It seemed all right. But later he thought of no less than seven devastating things he could have said. One was, "Oh really?"

His mind still on Alice, Jeremy stopped walking and looked down at his brogues. "Fine shoes," he murmured, his eyes dead. "Very fine shoes."

Wearing three pairs of socks was getting to be an awful drag, however, like Marcel Proust. Mostly because of keeping it a secret from Alice. Jeremy would just like to see her face if she found out, that's all.

He had decided that the shoes must go. He had spent quite a lot of time in planning ways of getting rid of the brogues. Most ways were too simple. He felt the need of something complex and crafty.

Now Jeremy walked on. Guilt-smudged, he reminded himself that Alice was an excellent cook.

He entered the copse where Fifi hunted smells with dithery tail. Around him thrust foliage, thumbs of a thousand gardeners saying let him live, let him live.

Jeremy drew in the green through eyes and nose. He smiled dreamily. He slowed, touched the trees he passed. "Simba," he whispered. "Umgowa."

In one of his secret, private worlds, Jeremy Wood was Tarzan.

He strolls the jungle trail, a magnificent male of tallness and rippling steellike muscles, of broad shoulders and narrow hips, of a loincloth whose frontal, mammoth bulge makes Jane tremble and pant. He moves with his magnificent head high. He is ever alert to danger. Nothing eludes the darting gaze of his magnificent eyes. And lo, suddenly, from above comes a slithery sound. King Cobra looking for a victim, mayhap? Little does the serpent know that his master is magnificently below, keen to do battle, his head craning eagerly upward in search of the enemy, craning and twisting. . . .

Fifi yapped.

Back on Hampstead Heath, Jeremy hurried out of the copse. His neck ached.

Fifi was nearby. Rigid, a foreleg raised, she was playing at setter. Her recipients, a young man and his girl, were walking past, hand in hand. Jeremy watched the couple as he slowed. He tensed his stomach.

Jeremy had a special, acute antenna tuned to people's reactions to his dog. If they said "What a darling little thing!" he was blasé. If they gave condescending smiles, he became furious. The latter emotion he usually managed to pin on some other aspect of the condescenders. He was not aware of his love for Fifi. Were he ever to become so aware, he would have sublimated the fact. That the dog and her need for walks were the bane of his life was important to him.

After flitting Fifi an indifferent glance, the young couple walked on by. Jeremy relaxed and went in the other direction.

"Come on," he called, and added, just in case, "You silly-looking thing." He glanced back. It was all right.

Massaging his neck, Jeremy hummed as he strolled and tried to imagine Alice trembling and panting.

Presently he switched back to grumble. He mused that no matter what happened, Alice would not get the upper hand. Which, of course, was what she wanted. Oh yes. She'd like him to do little chores, take her up snacks on a tray when she was in bed. Scurry scurry. Not that she'd ever said she'd like snacks on a tray in bed. But you could tell. She'd like him to do all kinds of things. Jump to it every time she cleared her throat. But no. Oh no. He would continue to be the boss of the house. He would *not* play bridge, he would *not* join the Young Conservatives, he would *not* get involved with her charities.

Oh no. Not likely. Any trousers to be worn, he would do the wearing.

Abruptly, Jeremy spoke aloud. "A tramp came to the door," he said. "Looking for old clothes. Trousers and stuff. You know. The way they do. Tramps. I hadn't got anything to give, but then he looked down at my shoes. Wistful. So there you are. It was foolish of me really."

Nodding approval at the ploy, Jeremy rounded a clump of high bushes.

Fifi was with another dog. She and the fat brown mongrel were nose to nose in communication, with quivers, like Eskimos at a bow-and-arrow hunt meeting.

Jeremy knew the dog. Called Rover, it belonged to a man whom Jeremy thought of, totally without whimsy, as Rover's father. He was one of the two score people Jeremy knew by sight from his Heath walks and who were thought of by him as connexions of the names they called out.

The two men had seen each other perhaps three hundred times over the past five years, and had often passed close. One evening, fired by a glorious sunset, they had exchanged nods.

Rover's father appeared around the bushes. He was cavorting a walking stick. This he subdued to the regulation swing-stab on catching sight of Jeremy.

The men drew closer together and Jeremy didn't know what to do with his eyes.

He wondered how it would look if he were to start bounding

around in a circle. He would put his arms at his sides, his feet together, and just bound.

Yes. Lovely. Rover's father would be shocked and staggered and aware of him.

Jeremy smiled, thrilled. Unconscious of the fact that he had come to a stop, he stared inward with fascination at a film clip of himself bounding in a circle.

"Dog or a bitch?"

Jeremy came alert. Unflapping his arms from his sides, he told Rover's father, who stood six feet away, "A bitch. They won't fight."

"No. That's true. They won't."

"And she's been spayed."

"The best thing."

"Yes."

The man grinned. "Take away the nursery and leave the playpen, eh?"

Jeremy had heard it six million times. He laughed.

Both men glanced at the dogs and glanced away again from the scene of rear sniffs. Jeremy said, "She's been spayed."

"Poppy's too old anyway," the man said.

Jeremy's breath caught. He was unnerved. His face snapping to expressionless, he slammed out, "I thought his name was Rover."

"Oh it is. It is. It certainly is. Yes. Rover. Indeed. Good old Rover. But sometimes we call him Poppy."

The man was blushing.

Relaxing, Jeremy allowed his eyelids to sag in a superior, bartender way. He saw the truth of the matter. Poppy was the dog's real name. It had never in its life been Rover.

Jeremy looked at Poppy's father with new eyes, permitting sympathy in a lordly, unheated manner while denying a feeling of kinship.

He had been in his early forties for a long time, was that type who enters middle-age from school, as if feeling there is something immature about youth. Stocky, high-shouldered, he wore a blue serge suit complete with weskit. The knot in his tie was incredibly small; looking painfully tight under the outbulging neck, it might have been created by a corset-string puller of fanatic skill. His lapels were curly.

The man had a round pink face of squashed features, the nose a wart with holes, mouth a bottom lip pushed high, eyes like blue water. His close-cut kinky hair was rusty, the colour of a pianist's face when he tries Bach after a year in tonking.

A slave, Jeremy thought, seeing a man who was plain, soft, and watery, a man like a sausage tied in the middle. Jeremy could almost picture the snack being taken upstairs on a tray.

"Rover," the man said.

"Quite so."

"Good name for a dog. Rover."

"I couldn't agree more," Jeremy said, sagging slightly at the knees to convey sincerity.

The man lifted his high shoulders. "Well."

"Yes," Jeremy said.

Passing each other with unattractive smiles, they went on. They called to their dogs without using names.

A slave, Jeremy thought.

It was as clear as could be. Poor sod. Owned by a hard woman with thin lips. Shrill voice too, probably. Made him walk an ugly old mongrel with a giggly name. Poppy, for heaven's sake.

Jeremy shook his head.

He would never be reduced to that. Too proud and strong. He walked Fifi because, being a reasonable and fairly intelligent man, he realised he couldn't have *everything* his own way, had to . . .

Glancing up at the sinking sun and giving a lying thought to how hot it was, Jeremy loosened the knot of his tie, drew it down, and unbuttoned his collar. He pulled the knot farther down. Last, he freed the tie ends from their clip and let them dangle.

His walk took on the faintest of swaggers. He glanced down at himself slyly. He felt almost quite the rogue.

All through this he hadn't stopped thinking of Alice. Now he was scraping along on:

. . . Why, she even spied on him when he took Fifi out!

Jeremy gaped. His mouth sagged like the seat of old pants, his eyes became marbles that had lost many a match, and his shoulders oozed forward, pulled by arms grown simianly long.

The astonishment was an act that he returned to time and again.

Spied on, he mused. It was as plain as day. She wanted to catch him up to no good, get something on him so that she could use it as a rod of control. The . . . the *rapacity* of it was astounding.

Jeremy went into a semigape.

Not for the gift of height would he have correctly recalled that Alice had followed him on only three occasions. Not for the outright present of a mammoth bulge at the front would he have acknowledged those occasions as being to his advantage.

Alice had come openly to find him. Once to report a telephone call: wholesaler wanting half a gross of the three-legged elm. Once with a telegram: his offer for the Bedford factory had been accepted. Once to remind him of television: a play he wanted to see was scheduled for imminent showing.

Watched, Jeremy thought. Lurked behind. Slinked after. Or slunk. Trailed in shadows. Observed through binoculars. Alice was determined to find a lever with which to prise him into the corner. A waste of time. As were all her machinations. He was the big wheel, impervious to cogs. There would be no slavery, no jumping to it, no scurry scurry.

Gape over, Jeremy smiled.

He continued across Hampstead Heath. Tie dangling, he strolled for another thirty minutes. He saw the mothers of Diddles, Winky, and Snootums, also Pom-Pom's sister, also the fathers of Nero, Brute, Fang, and Wolf. He enjoyed the air and the brutality of Alice. He threw sticks for Fifi.

As always on these outings, Jeremy was content.

Like the career of an honest politician, Horsetrough Lane was stunted. A double row of terraced houses eked its hundred yards. One end dashed sharply, with relief, into a street of villas; the other end opened onto the Heath.

Fifty years before, the flat-faced, gardenless houses had been the homes of labourers. Nowadays, only those parenthesised in a painful tax bracket could afford the rent or purchase price.

There had been a commensurate change in appearance. The gloomy brickwork was hidden under white stucco, unusable shutters hung at the windows, and doors were painted bright topical colours or the matt black of the meaningful individualist.

What Horsetrough Lane had lost in gritty character, it had gained in being something to smile at; but pleasantly. The street meant well.

Number twelve had yellow shutters and a blue door and a shy trickle of ivy. From brass-bound tubs siding the step, geraniums floundered as wildly as Faulkner's syntax. Above were antique carriage lamps, chromed. The three windows—one down, two up —were backed with lace curtains backed with venetian blinds.

The exterior of number twelve suggested fancifully that had there been a lawn, it would have owned plaster gnomes—though something close to the genuine, perhaps made in Zurich.

The blue door opened directly into the living room. The only room downstairs apart from the kitchen, it was narrow and deep, like a spinster philosopher. It had been created by removal of walls between pokey front parlour and back, plus the wall that separated these from the hall. Now the stairs were open to the whole and light came in from the windows at both ends.

An attractive room. It was also clean and neat, yet not so far gone in the latter as to be a nuisance.

There were large bookcases and a small TV, chintz-cosseted furniture, hearth logs behind which lay a light-bulb coated with orange nail varnish, pretty drapes, and Monet prints. There was a plain red fitted carpet like one of those days in a bloodbank.

The french windows at the rear looked out onto what had been called a backyard, had become a garden, was presently a patio, and would any day now be a leisure area. The original outhouse lavatory had been made into a bar. Underfoot was crazy-paved. Ivy threshed. There were white chairs that spent most of their time in dampness.

Thirty feet away, beyond the knee-high wall, was the rear window of another house. It stared across brazenly: the mutually owned trellis that gave privacy had blown down two years before and was awaiting replacement: the neighbours concerned couldn't make up their minds between Georgian design and Grecian.

The question was being discussed now, placidly, by Alice Wood and Mr. Barlow. They were in their own patios. As often happened, they had wandered outside to chat.

Alice, wearing a light summer dress, stood comfortably with one foot up on the low wall, and Mr. Barlow kept dropping his walking stick.

"Them Greeks," he said.

"Yes."

"It'd be encouragement, in a way."

Alice shook her head. "This has nothing to do with modern politics. It's ancient design."

"Thin end of the wedge, me dear."

"Do you think so?"

"I do."

"Well, perhaps you have a point there."

"Oh, I don't know. I wouldn't say that."

Mr. Barlow's present mind had little in it of Greece. He was wondering how soon he could drop his stick again in order to have another look at Alice's drawers.

The Woods' backing neighbour was sixty years old. He had a bent, arthritic body. He smelled of liniment and fried bacon. Despite a widower's loneliness and the pain of his affliction, he had a cheery mien.

Many-spoked wheels with concentric rims had been pressed into the dark putty around his eyes, themselves alert and restless, like young insomnia. His nose was a beak, his mouth a permanent pucker of judiciousness. His cheeks and chin were sabered by the unbeatable opponent. He had hirsute ears; atop his head, hair was as nonexistent as inspiration.

"Grecian," Alice murmured, to keep things going. She was thinking about dinner.

"Oh, I shouldn't think so," Mr. Barlow said, wondering away.

"All bits and bobs."

"Certainly."

A retired tailor, Mr. Barlow always wore thick, shapeless, shabby tweeds, as if in refutation, or relief, the way a chef will go home to fish and chips. Under his jacket he wore an overlarge Arran Island sweater, the gaping circular neckline of which sometimes got in his mouth. Wintertimes he added an overcoat with a hot-water bottle in each pocket. Even so, he always looked cold.

Mr. Barlow was fond of Mr. and Mrs. Wood, particularly

Alice. His feelings for her were mostly avuncular; but he did enjoy the views of her intimacy.

Undeniably, Alice was pretty.

She had an open, naive face with pert, pouty lips. Her blue gaze was steady. The face seemed to have been created five minutes ago—it had that freshness, that animation.

This vitality continued through Alice's body. She was a small person, neatly put together, cute. Her slender figure had firmness and roundness. Overall, Alice Wood was a quiet delight.

"Now you take the Georgian," Mr. Barlow said.

"It's such a vague period."

"Me dear, 1740 to 1830. Nothing vague about that."

"No. But you know."

"Forthright and sturdy design."

"Well," Alice said. She had the suspicion, coming back from thoughts of dinner, that they were arguing on the wrong sides. It would not be the first time.

"Sturdy," Mr. Barlow said. "No nonsense with them Georges."

Alice sighed. "It's quite a problem, I'm afraid."

Mr. Barlow dropped his stick.

His nervousness, Alice knew, came from the fact that he thought they might actually reach an agreement. He need not have worried. Alice had no intentions of cutting him off with a new trellis. Being semihousebound, he needed the company of seeing his neighbours in their living room, needed the waves and chats and cups of tea.

A pleasant practicality lived in easy comradeship with Alice's naiveté, which, in any case, was not so much an inability to scent what was bad, more a disinclination to try. She was remarkably free of neuroses.

Mr. Barlow had recovered his stick but was still down on one knee. His head was oddly slanted. He seemed to be listening to the ground.

Alice asked, "Are you all right?"

"Mm?"

"All right?"

"Oh, yes," he said. "Yes yes. Lovely."

"That hip of yours."

"What? It's nothing, nothing at all."

A martyr, Alice thought. A silent sufferer. She said, "You're so brave."

"This bending does it good, see."

Alice looked away from the martyrdom. She examined the other trellises, which stretched away at either side, laid end to end like unsurprising epigrams.

"Not one other trellis," she said in the bright tone of discovery, "is Georgian."

"Oh?"

"It gives one pause."

"Quite so. Pause."

Alice swung her upraised leg thoughtfully from side to side. She became aware that Mr. Barlow was whimpering. Putting her foot down in order to lean over, she asked:

"Sure you're all right?"

He grunted and began to get up.

Alice put her hands behind her pertly. "Tell you what, let's leave the subject till the end of the summer, and then have a good natter about it. Okay?"

Mr. Barlow said, "Agreed."

They parted.

Back in her kitchen, a place of gleam, Alice got on with preparations for dinner. Already she had forgotten the stillborn trellis. Whatever the motives for or against, Alice would not have been overly concerned. Matters of that nature touched her only on the outer pole of her emotions, barging past ineffectually. Nothing stood a chance of more than a casual embrace in that arena dominated by her husband.

To Alice, Jeremy was all. She loved him. He was Number One, every other aspect of life a cracked zero. Far back in their marriage she had given up trying to get him involved in her interests; partly because she realised he had his work, mainly because those interests had lost their importance in the presence of Number One.

"They got burnt," Jeremy said.

He was by himself, walking along Horsetrough Lane. Fifi had been put back on her leash. Jeremy's collar was buttoned, his tie knot up in place.

He said, "I sat by this fire, you see, Alice. Talking to some Boy Scouts. I didn't realise how close I was to the embers. Before I knew what had happened, my shoes were . . ."

Jeremy gave his head a curt shake.

No good. Wouldn't work for a minute. Anyone at all, even Alice, would know you'd feel the heat before the damage was done.

Jeremy sneered, arching a nostril. He was glad he had never been a Boy Scout.

Reaching number twelve, he got out his key and let himself in. Fifi pulled free. She went yapping around the room, jumped on and off the furniture, made a brief, vicious attack on her security toy, a stuffed penguin; and finally, silent, threw herself into a blanketed corner and lay as still as death.

Alice came in from the kitchen. "Hello, darling."

"Hello, love."

"I thought I heard you."

"That was Fifi."

"Have a nice walk?"

"Would have had but for the snow drifts."

"Yes," Alice said, flicking a polite smile.

"And the wolves."

Alice put the tip of a forefinger in the middle of her top lip. "I hope you'll like it. I'm not sure about the sauce."

"You never disappoint me, love."

"Thank you."

Alice had gone back into the kitchen. Jeremy sat on the couch. He read his letters and skimmed the evening newspaper's headlines. Last, he opened *Punch* to its classified section at the back.

His three-line advertisement was a standing insert, unchanged over the past two years. Nevertheless, Jeremy checked it every week. The copy above his shop address read NOW IS THE TIME TO THINK OF OUTDOOR FURNITURE! SEND FOR OUR COLOURED BROCHURE.

Reading it now, Jeremy felt the mild thrill of guilt. The advertisement was a lie. Weekly he decided it must be changed and told himself he would do it first thing. Lying was immoral; the world had quite enough dishonesty already.

The literature Jeremy sent out in answer to enquiries was in black and white. *There was no coloured brochure.*

There never had been. The project died when, his copy already placed, Jeremy received the estimates of plain and coloured.

Almost daily in his shop Jeremy had the distant and exciting dread that a letter would come, or an ex-would-be customer, or a detective from the Fraud Squad; come to accuse grimly, "Your brochure is not coloured."

As the kitchen door swung outward, Jeremy quickly tossed *Punch* aside. Alice appeared carrying two gin and tonics.

You don't know what I go through, Jeremy thought.

Alice sat on the couch; sat close. She and Jeremy held hands for a moment and smiled. They sipped their drinks. Alice took a cigarette from the silver box on the coffee table, Jeremy reached for the silver lighter. He lit her cigarette. He didn't smoke himself, had never felt in need of the crutch. There was always Tarzan.

Alice said, "I've been talking to Mr. Barlow."

"Yes?"

"About the trellis."

Jeremy clenched his toes.

She's at it again. Here she goes. We're in for it now. Nag nag. She'll come back to it time after time until I give in and have an argument with the poor old sod. So she thinks.

Jeremy sipped his drink. Alice continued to talk about the trellis, making conversation. She was conscientious in pressing her belief that a man should not bring his work home with him. In any case, Jeremy's business was over her head. To Alice, all rustic furniture looked alike.

"It'll work itself out," Jeremy said.

Nodding, Alice leaned back. She folded her arms, tapped one foot, and fretted about having put in too much salt.

Folds arms, Jeremy thought. Taps foot. He enjoyed the assumption that Alice was quietly fuming her way through this latest setback.

"I must check on the dinner."

Alone, Jeremy smiled. His slow-roving gaze met not the conspirator it wanted, but the bookshelves. Jeremy remembered.

He rose, went to a shelf, and drew out a dictionary. He flipped pages with the vague pretence that he wasn't looking for "rapacity."

He found it anyway. Returning the book to its slot after reading the definition, he told himself he had been near enough. Not that it mattered.

Back at the coffee table, he stood to finish his gin and tonic. He put down the empty glass and said, "That's better." He always said it. It was as comforting as the drink.

He strolled down the room, legs loose. At the front corner opposite the staircase, he turned and leaned against the wall. He closed the eye on that side, thus blotting out the wall. One-eyed, he surveyed the room. It appeared vast.

Jeremy spent quite a lot of time in this corner. He preferred the view to the one from the nearby front window, which was of the houses close across the street, and which made him uneasy after a while. Looking out, he always became filled with a mystic sadness, like longing in the young.

Enjoying cyclopian vastness, his fore-clasped hands twiddling their thumbs slowly and without collision, Jeremy stayed in his corner until dinner was served.

They ate at the table near the french windows. Alice fussed. She settled to her own food only when Jeremy had crinkled his eyes in approval, like a grammarian at an error.

The braised steak had aplomb, charm, and an underlying note of character; the red wine was medium rare.

Jeremy talked of his satisfaction with the van he had bought recently (NO CHARGE FOR DELIVERY IN THE GREATER LONDON AREA it said on the shop window and in the Yellow Pages), of the famous actor he had seen in the Baker Street tube station this evening, of the profit differential between his two-seater with the knotty back and his old-gnarled three with the in-bent arms.

Smiling as she ate, Alice listened and felt proud of her husband's worldliness. She reminded herself, however, that Jeremy should be steered away from business.

Over cheese and biscuits, Alice said, "There'll be another meeting soon."

"What?"

"You know, dear. The Horsetrough Lane Residents Association."

Here we go, Jeremy thought with resignation. Not a moment's peace. Bloody Horsetrough Lane Res Ass. She's a sticker, you've got to say that for Alice.

He said, "Is that so?"

"Yes, dear."

"Well now."

"We might go along to the meeting if we're not doing anything."

Cunningly neutral, Jeremy asked, "What's the new clamour?"

"Isn't one. We're still bombarding the council."

Jeremy thought: Clever, that *we*.

"They'll never pull it off," he said. "They think they will, but they have to see they haven't an earthly chance."

"Time will tell," Alice said.

The Residents Association had decided that their street should have another name—Horsetrough Lane was coarse and farmyardy. They had written to the local council, suggesting "Heathview Mall." Receiving a negative response, they had next sent a petition with sixty-two signatures. A deputation of four had followed.

"The thing I like about the Bedford factory," Jeremy said neatly, if cruelly, "is using it as a base for adverts in northern newspapers."

He reminded himself, in passing, that those advertisements read SEND FOR OUR BROCHURE.

Alice said, "Yes, darling."

"It reduces the freight charges tremendously, shipping the stuff out from there. It's an added attraction."

"It might be an idea to go along to that meeting."

"A great attraction."

"After all," Alice said, "you're the one who founded the association."

Unfair. Low blow. Foul. A dirty rotten trick. How could such an otherwise sweet person have this vicious side? Easy. It was that mad lust for power.

"Remember, dear?"

"That," Jeremy said, "was when I was innocent. I didn't know we'd be caught up in all these cocktail parties."

"There's only been one so far this year."

"I always get stuck with that awful Twittleton woman."

"Whittleton."

"She's a cat maniac. Pussy mad."

Alice looked as though she wasn't sure if she should blush or not. She said, "Still."

Jeremy leaned forward, smiling. "A wonderful meal, love," he said, seeing not Alice but himself on a streetcorner with in addition to the usual accoutrements, a large lapel button bearing the initials HLRA.

He was still smiling and seeing what would never be, when a noise from the kitchen told him Alice had gone from her seat.

Jeremy went to sprawl on the couch. Like the ears of gossip-fodder, his face was pink and glowing: wine, food, victory.

He read the evening newspaper.

Presently, Alice came in with coffee, plus a brandy for her husband. Between sips, Jeremy read out items from the paper. On the political front, he explained the niceties Alice didn't understand, and those he didn't understand himself he said she wouldn't understand.

"I do wish you'd go in for it," Alice said. "All that knowledge going to waste."

Feeling secure enough not to fight, or to switch away, or to think, Jeremy buried it up to the nostrils with, "Perhaps when I'm older."

"Mm."

"You know. More the family man."

They exchanged a shy, secret-sharing smile. It had the light embarrassment of unplanned alliteration.

When Alice was thirty-five, it had been decided, she would stop taking the Pill. There would follow Adrian and Jennifer, who would always be sweet and about four years old.

Jeremy finished his coffee and brandy. Alice switched on the television set and stared at a commercial, rapt and believing.

Jeremy got up and strolled to the front window. Hands clasped behind, he teetered on his toes while looking out at Horsetrough Lane through the venetian blinds.

The wine and brandy had Jeremy in a mild thrash. He felt like doing something, preferably something reckless. He felt like going somewhere. He felt like making his existence known.

"Darling," Alice said. "This is that new series. It's awfully funny."

Jeremy sighed and turned with condescension for those who went in for vicarious living.

He soon became involved in the situation comedy. He laughed at the neurotic characters. Alice, beside him, shared the enjoyment. Every time they laughed they touched each other.

The evening sauntered to a close.

Alice yawned. Jeremy tickled her in the ribs. Giggling and blushing, she returned the tickle. The message had been given and received both ways: tonight was sex night.

The Woods' lovemaking always began with tickling. Sometimes the preliminary was subdued and giggly, as now. Sometimes it was uproarious, a chase around the house.

Now, after scuffling on the couch for a minute, Jeremy and Alice turned out lights, locked doors, said good night to Fifi, and went chuckling upstairs to toothbrushes and bed.

The life of Jeremy Wood had a dangerous tranquility.

TWO

In rubber boots, brown corduroys, and a sweater, Jeremy was as unlikely as morning suicide in his surroundings, the platform of an Underground station, the urban ultimate.

Stretched out beside the drop to the rails were a hundred other people. Some were pacing. Jeremy too would have liked to pace, but he knew he would bring attention to himself by the whistling of his corduroys.

The train racketed in. Jeremy got aboard and out of unconscious habit found a seat where he wouldn't need not to look at anyone.

He remembered the time he had taken a shotgun to work. Unusable, destined for wall display, he had carried it broken over his arm. He had stood there in the middle of the carriage, aware of eyes while he nonchalantly scanned advertisements. Once he had yawned. He had gone three stops past Baker Street.

This morning he was carrying an overnight bag. Today being Thursday, he would go from work to Bedford and spend the night there. He was pleased with the prospect, as always. His weekly trips were little adventures. Anything could happen. Nothing ever had, really. But still.

At Baker Street, Jeremy left the train and went up to street level.

The morning was fine and mild. Jeremy set off walking. He felt confident and young and unencumbered, like an art student without talent.

Wood's Rustic Furniture was two countrified bow windows with a nail-studded door between. On the pavement were samples of the wares. Inside was a disorderly jumble of three-seaters and in-bent arms, knotty backs and old-gnarleds.

The shop was already in operation when Jeremy arrived. Tom Barr had gone off delivering in the van, and the other staff member was by the desk at the rear.

"Good morning, Mrs. Hendon," Jeremy said. "Good morning, good morning."

"Good morning, sir."

Averting his eyes from a pile of brochures, Jeremy asked, "What are you up to, Mrs. Hendon?"

"I'm sorting the mail, sir," the woman said, implying but not adding "Obviously."

"Ah yes. Yes."

Mrs. Hendon had a briskness that her employer found intimidating. He countered this by being unnecessarily jovial, and by inventing reasons to give her bonuses.

Mrs. Hendon was fifty years old. She had a thin body but a large and weighty-looking head. A mistake seemed to have been made somewhere. She was as wrong as the Lord's Prayer on a pin-table.

Her face was broad and flat, spread out by need. She had silver hair dragged back into a bun, a sweet smile, and killer eyes. She was an excellent saleswoman. Also a first-rate supervisor and secretary. Her rough tweeds struck the right note.

Mrs. Hendon would have been perfect, in Jeremy's view, were it not for her sharp voice and the alarm she caused him whenever she nodded. She was a flawed gem.

"We're somewhat late this morning," she said.

"Well, I walked part of the way."

"Indeed."

Jeremy spent an hour over top-level letters. Other paperwork he left for Mrs. Hendon to handle; she became brisk to a frighteningly mechanical degree when, preoccupied, he left nothing for her attention.

Jeremy helped serve customers until eleven, then went back to the large shed that was a combination garage and storeroom.

His driver/handyman was a youth of twenty. Silent, lanky, with greasy long hair, he had a sallow complexion and a shuddery, wet cough. He smoked incessantly. The seat of his coveralls sagged. He was in love with a motor bike. As far as Wood's Rustic Furniture was concerned, his chief value was ownership of a clean driving licence.

"Well," Jeremy said, rubbing invisible tobacco between his palms. "Well now."

Tom Barr smiled. He stopped preparing a chair for rail shipment, sat on it, and looked with keen interest at the ball of string he was holding.

Jeremy drooped. Persevering, he asked, "Get everything delivered all right?"

Tom Barr nodded, looked up, and nodded again. "Yes."

"Very good."

"Yes."

"No problems?"

"No."

A rose impaling itself on its own thorn, Tom Barr lit a cigarette.

"We mustn't go on chatting," Jeremy said quickly, before the coughing could begin. "Back to the treadmill, Tom."

A puzzled, wary look came into the youth's eyes. Jeremy returned drearily to the shop.

Until twelve-thirty he ambled, tended a lone customer who was looking for a friend, watched from behind cover Mrs. Hendon typing, tried various seats, and picked off bits of crunchy bark and then tried to stick them back on again with spit. He told himself he was not bored. Not in the least.

Ham rolls and beer cheered him in a nearby pub, as well as the bustle. He stretched out the lunch hour to eighty-four minutes.

Mrs. Hendon and three women were contemplating in silence a garden arch. Jeremy sidled past the group.

The afternoon's only event was the sale of twelve chairs with stressed backs. The buyer wanted cheapness, not charm.

At four-thirty, eager for his little adventure to begin, Jeremy got in the van with his overnight bag and set off.

He settled down to the two-hour journey. His gaze was sharp for signs of girl hitchhikers, early twenties, going home after a year of loose living in the city.

Stammering in sluggish traffic through the outer suburbs, he saw only people on their way home from work. He pitied them, the swarming sheep. What they needed was a good shaking up.

Jeremy wondered what effect it would have if he were to stop the van, get out, stand in the middle of the road, and shout.

He grinned. He pondered. The grin faded. The expression in his eyes edged into the penumbra of sadness.

He couldn't think what he would shout.

Jeremy Wood had been born in Bedford. His mother dying soon thereafter, he was put under the care of his paternal grandmother. Her recipe for successful child-rearing was love, abundant food, and a daily spoonful of Scott's Emulsion, which she called Scotch Emotion. She could write her own name quite neatly.

Short and stout and fussy, like a stemless flower, Mrs. Wood senior, wife of a carpenter, was determined that her son would get on. He had. He had become a literate cabinetmaker.

Mr. Wood shared his mother's determination. He worked long hours in order to send Jeremy to private schools so private that few people knew of their existence.

Jeremy was a dreamy boy. He spent a good deal of time staring out windows. He disliked walls. At home, he was happiest when his grandmother talked of her forester father; at school, when he was outdoors. He shone at nature study, reading, and watching sports.

He failed to get into a university, which, said his teachers, was because of spending too much time communing with Edgar Rice Burroughs.

With money borrowed from his disappointed father, he went to Australia and spent a contented year working on a sheep station. He flew home for his grandmother's funeral, and stayed on through his father's terminal illness.

At twenty Jeremy owned a business about which he knew nothing. The thought of selling out made him feel disloyal, like a better class of adulterer. Grey of mind, he put his soul to the grindstone.

When most of the skilled men had left him because of botched leadership, Jeremy got the brilliant idea of switching to rustic furniture. Craft would be secondary; he would be starting almost from scratch. It was a challenge. Jeremy was keen and excited. He never did pause to question why he had turned to this backward step in the woodworker's art.

He opened an outlet in London, he advertised, and he took a hand in manufacture. He prospered.

At this point in Jeremy's rise to success, he met Alice, daughter of a Bedford lumber merchant. They had similar backgrounds, though Alice's schools had been slightly less obscure than Jeremy's. They courted.

They walked, went to the pictures, necked in the workshop, talked politics and books. One night, Jeremy brought off an awkward and uncomfortable seduction on a three-seater knotty back. Guiltily, he proposed.

During the engagement they made love frequently and with increasing finesse, though Alice always insisted on total darkness. This, Jeremy suspected, was so that she would have no visual memory of the act, and could therefore pretend it had never happened.

Marriage accomplished, they moved to London and lived in a series of flats before buying the house in Horsetrough Lane. The business thrived. Jeremy dealt with the trade as well as with retail. He sold nationwide via mail order. He took over larger premises in Bedford.

Wood's Rustic Furniture became well established. The climb was over, the challenge gone. Jeremy lost interest.

In time, he sublimated his restlessness and vague longings into the imitation struggle for domestic supremacy. He was unfortunate in having a solid business, his own home, and an excellent marriage partner. But Jeremy didn't allow himself a running victory, which would have spoiled the ploy. He frequently gave in to the wishes he had created for Alice—and then invented more. Orwell would have understood.

To Jeremy, subjugation being a condition he abhorred, the struggle was real. He would have given it up only if he found a better battle.

★★★★★★

The factory was two Nissen huts surrounded by one yard of weed-dotted gravel. Flanking were a service station and a warehouse; opposite, shops of no ambition.

As identical outside as anyone's army inside, the Nissens' interiors were markedly different. One, a bedlam of untidiness like vacation minds, was Manufacture. The other was sedate Administration.

The six employees had gone when Jeremy arrived. He went into the office. After leaving his bag on a made-up cot in a back room, he returned to the desks and the paperwork that had been left for his inspection. That took half an hour. He went next door. That took five minutes.

Another five and he had locked up the factory and was standing outside. His corduroys he had changed for a pair of flannels, grey and silent.

Jeremy thought about what to do now.

He could go to see his in-laws, or call on his manager, or visit his cousin who had the bicycle shop, or go to the café. Or he could just wander off and do whatever he fancied.

Jeremy wandered off, feeling illicit. He ignored the fact that his in-laws were away on holiday, that he had never yet called on his manager or cousin, and that he hadn't eaten in that café for two years.

He walked past the suburb's lingering businesses, all closed. He looked brightly in shop windows, watched a dog chase a cat and didn't pick sides, and eyed covertly a pretty girl at a bus stop until she turned and eyed him back. He bought fish and chips, which he ate from the bag as he walked.

In the centre of town, everything was closed apart from cinemas and pubs. Jeremy strolled. For the benefit of the few people about, he wore an amused expression.

Jeremy insisted to himself that it was fun, this, just wandering off and doing whatever you fancied.

He went into a movie house, sat for ten minutes, and came out again. He was pleased by the reckless waste of money. He was grabbed by a bold idea: flushing with shock and self-admiration, he bought another ticket, went into the auditorium, sat for one minute, and then strolled out.

The only reason the usher didn't say anything, Jeremy knew, was because he was so startled. Same with the box-office girl, who at any rate was staring at him as he walked casually away. He could feel it.

Jeremy was wondering whether or not to do the same thing again, really shake them up, when he heard a crash of piano music. He was passing a pub.

He went in, musing that it might be fun to order an expensive drink and leave it. This he forgot on seeing a crowded and boisterous room. He smiled at it all as he sidled to the bar. Deferentially, he ordered a beer.

Everyone was in company and talking. Jeremy drank quickly and pretended not to be alone every time the barmaids glanced his way. He drank four more beers. His head began to ache with the roar of talk, the smoke, the piano music, and the effort of picking up bits of conversations.

Leaving the pub, he set off to walk muzzily back. He thought of Alice and home with a regret as profound as that of any bridge-burning emigrant. The ache went from his head to his throat.

At the factory he undressed swiftly, got into bed, and at once fell asleep. He dreamt tearfully of being surrounded by friends in the dressing room of a concert hall, where he had just concluded a piano concerto.

"It's two lumps for you, isn't it, Mr. Wood?"

"How nice of you to remember."

It was eleven o'clock the next morning. Jeremy and Miss Cox were having coffee and cakes in a tea shop that smelt of oven. There were plates on the walls, idling old ladies, and the mandatory despotic female owner with a mouth shaped for holding pins.

The secretary of Wood's Rustic Furniture said, "I can't decide which one to take." She bent over the plate of cakes. "There are so many."

"Spoilt for choice."

She looked up. "That's it, Mr. Wood. That's it exactly. I didn't think of that."

Jeremy was in a cheerful mood, like a bachelor wedding guest. He had enjoyed the respect of his employees earlier, the minor problems he had discussed with his manager, and the general approval of his new design for a lounging chair in old gnarled, knotty pine, or singed oak. He was now enjoying the trip out for elevenses with Miss Cox.

It had become a regular part of the Bedford visits. Jeremy always made a point of not mentioning it at home, though he did murmur cryptic allusions, while watching Alice from the corners of his eyes, to cakes and the pleasing intimacy of small cafés and the appetites of young girls.

Miss Cox was twenty-two. As slim and nervous as the hopes of compulsive losers, she had a sweet face behind large spectacles. Jeremy had often bet himself that she would be inclined to tremble and pant.

They each selected a cake. Gesturing, Jeremy talked expansively of Wood's Rustic Furniture's future growth. There would be a larger factory, modern, with offices on top, all glass and steel and efficiency. He thought it sounded horrible. He talked on nevertheless.

Miss Cox watched, a small V of a smile on her eating mouth.

Jeremy became a shade grander as he mused: Adoration. Plain old-fashioned adoration. That was what she . . . invoked.

He was talking about Factory No. 3, in Glasgow, seven stories tall, when Miss Cox interrupted. She put down her knife and fork in a manner that suggested a decision firmly made.

"Mr. Wood."

"Yes?"

She addressed the plate of cakes. "I've remembered something I have to do at home."

"I see."

She asked the plate, "I wonder if you could possibly drive me to the house?"

Jeremy's heart began to pound. Also looking at the plate, he thought: This is it. This is definitely it.

"Of course," he said hoarsely. "We'll go at once."

During the paying of the bill and the awkward walk back, all in silence, Jeremy told himself he would not go through with it.

He had never been unfaithful to Alice. He was not going to start now. He loved his wife. He was not about to have sordid affairs with every little secretary who flung herself at his head. Who needed sex with naked young girls in warm dim bedrooms at eleven o'clock in the morning while other people were sensibly at work and not knowing anything about it? Not Jeremy Wood. He had the mature strength to resist. He would say, at the house, "I'll wait for you here."

They got in the van and set off. Jeremy was still thrumming. He told himself he should prepare her now for the let-down.

"Nice day," he said.

"It is, Mr. Wood. Yes. A very nice day."

"Yes."

"Yes."

The house was a neat semidetached. Jeremy's first jolt came when Miss Cox said, opening the door, "I won't be a minute, Mr. Wood."

He reminded himself that she had her self-respect to consider.

"I'll come with you," he said.

"All right, Mr. Wood."

The second jolt was seeing the door opened by a third person. Jeremy's thrumming stopped.

The gooseberry was an older version of Miss Cox. The thought of group sex ran rapidly and plaintively through Jeremy's mind, like an exhibitionist in a nudist camp.

He was introduced to the mother. While Miss Cox went inside they talked of what a nice day it was. Jeremy wore a stark grin.

"Very nice," he said.

"Yes."

The secretary came out. She was carrying a gaily wrapped package. There was another bowing handshake and then they were back in the van, moving, and Miss Cox was saying: "It's for my boyfriend, Mr. Wood. It's his birthday. I'm meeting him at lunchtime and I'd've died if I'd forgotten it. I don't know how to thank you, Mr. Wood."

"Not at all," Jeremy said bitterly.

An hour later he was on the road back to London. He had declined his manager's invitation to lunch and hurried through remaining details of the visit.

Jeremy sat slumped at the wheel like flesh by a scar. He felt inordinately dreary. His little adventure was almost over.

Glancing aside at the greenery, he muttered, "Umgowa."

⁂

The Society for Distressed German Ponies, a nonprofit organization, had its headquarters in the president's home. The house was large and luxurious.

Miss Tomkin, however, had sturdy private means. Something

more than a tithe of her income went to the charity, and represented, in secret fact, nine tenths of the contributions.

Secret because Miss Tomkin would have been found dead in a man's bed rather than let it be known that her society was a flop. The SDGP was her baby, she loved it; she fed it well and gladly.

Machiavellian was Miss Tomkin's art. Using envelopes of forty different makes, which she kept in her bedroom, she sent herself sums of money ranging from one pound sterling to five, with an occasional tenner. The envelopes she addressed in a thrilling variety of disguised hands and posted every other morning from randomly chosen parts of London. On these outings, by taxi, she wore dark glasses.

Miss Tomkin was one of those tall thin Englishwomen who look part horse.

This Friday afternoon, she was pretending to read while watching Mrs. Wood.

Alice, at a desk, was opening envelopes. She held up the contents of the latest one, crying, "Another five-pound note!"

"Really?" Miss Tomkin mumbled, reading on.

Alice marvelled at how the president could stay so calm. This was in addition to the continuing, usual marvel that so many contributors wished to be anonymous.

"Aren't people wonderful, Miss Tomkin?"

"Yes, dear. Quite."

So staunch, so calm, so involved—Alice thought. She picked up another letter and shuffled herself comfortably.

Alice loved these weekly two-hour sessions. The room, of grand proportions, was a pleasing mixture of antiques and office equipment. The walls were dominated by arresting photographs of ponies: one on its knees by a pit-head, one being kicked by a brute of a man, one sagging under the weight of two fat women, one dead.

Being here made Alice feel soulful and worthy.

From an envelope she drew a slip of paper. It was a money order for twenty-five pence. She described it as she waved it in the air like a good-bye handkerchief.

Miss Tomkin swung around. "A *what?*" she gasped.

"A money order."

"Oh!"

"It's only for twenty—"

But Miss Tomkin had predatored forward and grabbed the paper. She was spurred into a showing of long teeth.

"How simply ripping!" the president said, making the exclamation point with a raised forefinger. Unnerved by success, she turned swiftly and left the room.

Alice gazed at the door with a wet smile. She understood. Dear Miss Tomkin. She could remain calm about large sums, for their size meant they came only from the purse—small sums came from the heart.

Meaningful and rewarding. That's what it was. It gave you so much. It warmed you all over like an electric blanket. Much more so than the Red Cross.

Alice felt disloyal to the Red Cross. She stopped thinking.

Tuesday mornings Alice spent at the mobile canteen depot (Hampstead Division). With a handful of others, she unrolled bandages for the rollers, talked about those who hadn't turned up today, and waited for disaster. (There had never been one yet.) Sometimes there was a fire. They would all go in the van and have an exciting time of it until the police told them to move on. Sometimes, keeping in practise, they would go to the East End in search of down-and-outers, and leave a row of skid marks on sighting a likely prospect, who would then be made to eat a sandwich and drink hot, sweet tea.

If Alice had a complaint against the Red Cross, it was that she got only a smock to wear, not a uniform. But Tuesdays were fun, even though she never felt worthy, soulful, or rewarded.

Miss Tomkin returned. Her eyes were red and she carried two cups of coffee. She said, hoarse like an overworked cantor:

"We're having trouble about June."

Remembering just in time that there was a month by that name, Alice nodded instead of asking what was wrong with her.

Miss Tomkin put down the cups. "I refer to Saturday the sixteenth, of course."

"Of course."

"Our flag day."

"Yes."

"Unfortunately," Miss Tomkin said in italics. "Unfortunately, a problem has been created by a certain person."

"You mean . . . ?"

"Yes."

She meant the president of Friends of Brighton Donkeys. This society, like dozens of others, dwelled locally. When odd things were born they went to live in Hampstead. It was London's southern California.

"You don't mean . . . ?"

"Yes, Mrs. Wood. Precisely. A certain person has chosen the same day to sell flags for her inferior beasts."

Alice pretended to herself that she hadn't heard that last bit. She hated racial intolerance. "Outrageous," she said, stirring her coffee with a vicious hand.

"Indeed it is, Mrs. Wood. That person knows full well I have had the sixteenth for many years."

"Of course she does."

"It's a deliberate attack."

"True," Alice said.

"One will retaliate, naturally."

A shiver of thrill knocked Alice's knees together. "How?"

Miss Tomkin sipped coffee before saying an icy, "Sabotage."

"Ooh."

"War is war, Mrs. Wood."

"Oh yes," Alice said. She thought: If only Jeremy knew what he was missing. The intrigue, the danger, the soulfulness and things. Alice remembered that Jeremy was slaving away in Bedford, and felt guilty for her pleasure, but couldn't stop it.

"A certain person," Miss Tomkin said, "whose murky past is her own business, far be it from me to gossip, *I* don't wish to bandy about the story of her association in April of 1947 with a petty officer, married with two children, and I know nothing about it anyway—and that certain person must realise I have powerful friends."

"Ah."

"Mr. Greenwood, the veterinary, now retired, went to school with my brother."

"Phew."

"And there are others."

Alice shook her head to show respect. She loved to see Miss Tomkin like this, full of fire and fight. Alice thought it could be because of the money order. She was glad she had sent it. She decided to send another next week.

"Sabotage," Miss Tomkin said.

Alice shuddered.

※※※※※※

The following evening, Jeremy came downstairs from changing his clothes and said, "I shan't bother taking Fifi out tonight."

This was because Alice had said, before he went upstairs, that Fifi had missed him on Thursday, which statement Jeremy had worked on diligently until it became: "You're being unfair to the unfortunate animal. Taking her out is *your* job. You don't really need to go to Bedford every damned week. You can damned well make up for it. Change your clothes quickly and get her out on that Heath."

There were a number of answers Jeremy could have given, and he gave them all to the bathroom mirror. The one he settled on was, "Don't tell *me* what to do."

When, however, he came down, he produced a new one, which he considered devastating in its mildness and total rejection.

"I shan't bother taking Fifi out tonight."

Alice was ironing. She said, "As you like, dear. It does look as though it might rain."

"That's what I thought," Jeremy said, his voice low. He was speaking for Alice's ears only, not his own.

"Was everything all right upstairs? You were an awfully long time."

Jeremy tightened his jaw muscles like they do in the movies. I'll stay upstairs all bloody night if I feel like it, and if I don't feel like it I won't.

He said, "I was thinking about things. Business. You know."

"This collar's just about had it," Alice said.

Jeremy went to the front window. He looked up at the sky. Boldly, and in a loud voice, he said, "No, it won't rain."

"That's good."

"I'll have a little walk in town. Look at the shops."

"All right, darling."

Sweating slightly, Jeremy left the house.

In ten minutes he was strolling the narrow, winding, downhill street. He felt masterly and sorry for Fifi. He saw a picture in black and grey of a leash hanging dust-coated from a nail below a sign that read GONE BUT NOT FORGOTTEN.

"You're being silly," he said aloud.

As Jeremy believed that the second sign of insanity was not answering yourself when spoken to, he said, "Very."

The street was quiet, sparse in people and cars. The shops were closed.

When Jeremy saw a group of people waiting at a bus stop, he was taken by a curious notion. It was the last in a series of thoughts.

First he mused on how awkward his shoes felt on the incline, even three-socks full; next, that it was mild enough this evening to go barefoot; next, how stuffily respectable those people were; last, what would they do if he were to take his shoes and socks off?

It was a thrilling notion. The people were so *English*. Stopping, Jeremy observed closely. The three men and two women were all middle-aged, all soberly dressed, all rigid of spine. They were standing neatly facing front and not talking.

Excited, Jeremy moved swiftly to the doorway of a shop. He feared that if he hesitated he would change his mind. He sat on the step and pulled off the shoes without undoing their laces. Each triple layer of hose he stripped off in one go. He rolled up the bottoms of his trousers so that the view would be unobstructed.

He rose. With jittery fingers he stuffed socks into shoes; then cradled the shoes on his chest where they couldn't possibly be missed. The pavement was warm.

Feeling wild, insane, a total rebel, Jeremy walked toward the bus stop. His face was flushed, and his eyes were unnaturally bright.

I'm doing it, he thought in terror and glee and disbelief. I'm really doing it.

He reached the queue. Stopping, he stood at its back, behind the centre-holder, a man with homburg and briefcase.

Jeremy was trembling. He gave notice of his presence by clearing his throat loudly. The sound came out with the high, wailing pitch of near-hysteria.

The people looked around. Every eyebrow was already raised over a downstretched eyelid; in defence.

Grinning fiercely, Jeremy read trauma from face to face.

Every person reacted in kind. He or she noted the shoes, snapped a worried glance downward, had the worry confirmed, winced at the solecism of having been crude enough to look, and turned firmly away.

The spines of the five increased their rigidity. Otherwise, nothing had changed.

Jeremy sagged.

He was not aware of producing another whine, one with the inflection of enquiry, supplication.

Nothing changed.

Mothering the shoes to his chest like slighted twins, Jeremy turned and moved on. He felt dazed.

Only distantly was Jeremy conscious of a passing girl and a giggle; and of his slump at the knees to lower his trouser bottoms.

Next thing he knew, he was standing in front of a man. The man said, "I say." It was the impressed tone in the voice that brought Jeremy alert.

He recognised Rover's father, his fellow dog-walker, on the Heath: pink squashed face, rusty-kinky hair, blue serge suit, and a tie with an overtight knot.

Jeremy mumbled a bleary, "Hello."

"That's all right," the man said. "I like that." There was envy and reproach in the admiration.

Jeremy straightened. He managed to collect himself enough so that he could display an air of faint boredom. He said, "Yes."

"Feet all right, are they?"—worried.

Jeremy, piqued: "Certainly. Of course."

Relieved and reproachful: "There you are."

"I simply felt like doing it," Jeremy said. "That's all."

Rover's father began to nod. When he had finished, he asked, "Know what you are?"

"What?"

"An anarchist."

Jeremy preened. Then he blushed for himself and subsided. He murmured, "Oh well."

Rover's father, confidential: "I'm a bit of an anarchist myself." And jutting back with a sealed-lip smile.

"Good," Jeremy said. He warmed to the man. He forgave him the knot in his tie.

"There aren't many of us."

"Very true."

"Tell you what," Rover's father said, pressing the spread fingers of both hands to his paunch. "I'll buy you a drink."

Jeremy felt cozy and large. He said, "Good show. Hold on a sec."

While leaning against a shop window to put on his shoes and socks, and while sending glances of pity toward the unseeing five at the bus stop, Jeremy exchanged names and particulars.

Mastin. Henry Mastin. Forty-two next birthday. All his own teeth. Insurance broker. Office in town. The little woman, Mona, was one of the best, one of the best. He used to have a rustic chair himself, in the old back garden. No kids. There was Rover.

Shod, Jeremy stood erect. He was now almost normal emotionally. However, he still had that glow of pride wrought by the other man's respect and awe.

He said jauntily, "Come along, old man."

The pub was all Edwardian elegance, spindles and wriggles and tassels, like an aged harlot. The place smelt of Indian carpet. There was a young-evening thinness of custom.

"What'll it be?" Jeremy asked at the bar. Aside, he gave the barmaid a smooth, "Good evening." It came off so well his ego was boosted further.

He leaned an elbow on the bar, tilted up his chin, and looked at Henry Mastin, who said:

"No no, Wood. This is on me."

Jeremy inclined his head. "Very well. Scotch and soda."

"I'll have the same."

Served, the two men nodded glasses at each other and sipped. Jeremy covered the shudder caused by the drink by dithering his shoulders and murmuring, "Chilly tonight."

For him, whisky was a rarity. He didn't like the taste. But anything other than Scotch would have sounded effete and jarring.

Henry Mastin was talking about insurance. "Boring," Mastin

said, putting down his empty glass. "Not for the likes of you and me. Not for anarchists."

Jeremy nodded.

Henry Mastin shucked one shoulder, as if dislodging a small animal, or the hand of restraint. He said: "Last week, Wood. Last week." He smiled reminiscently.

"Yes?" Jeremy asked, not looking worried.

"In the Underground it was."

Coldly: "Well?"

Hurrying now, Mastin said, "I'm standing there among all the sheep. I'm there alone in the centre bit. Everyone's as quiet as anything. Suddenly, I shout."

"Oh?"

"I shout as loud as I can."

"Er—what?"

"The world will end tomorrow!"

Jeremy didn't believe him for a moment. He drained his glass at a gulp and, before turning away, said. "Not bad, old man." With moist eyes he signalled the barmaid for a refill.

Jeremy thought furiously. He chose, rejected, reconsidered. Fresh drink in hand, he turned. His chin went up. He said, "The first time I streaked."

Mastin stiffened. He looked frowningly into his glass, as if at a fly.

"Across Piccadilly Circus," Jeremy said, inspired and flushed. At the same time, he was worrying his memory for details of what he had read about streakers.

"I wore nothing but my hat," he said. "You always wear a hat."

Henry Mastin shot a grim look at the top of Jeremy's head. "Oh really?"

Jeremy said, "I took one with me especially."

"Ah."

"It was a black bowler with a green feather at the side."

Mastin's face creased into near-capitulation. "What happened?"

"The wife was quite annoyed."

Henry Mastin gave in. He gaped his awe. "Your wife was with you," he said. "Christ."

"Quite annoyed. Wouldn't talk to me afterwards, when I escaped from him."

"Him?"

"The policeman."

"Christ."

"Didn't bother me though, Alice not talking. I'm the boss in my house."

Mastin gabbled, "Oh yes. So am I. Me too. Boss. Quite right. Christ." He emptied his glass.

Like a dictator, Jeremy became benevolent in security. He said, "Shouting in the Underground. That's all right."

Mastin brightened. "Yes."

"Takes nerve."

"A bit."

Jeremy finished his whisky and looked at his watch.

They walked to the door and went out onto the wide step, where they paused.

"We must do this again sometime," Mastin said.

Jeremy nodded. He was feeling dizzy and slightly nauseated; and he was smiling. That he had streaked across Piccadilly Circus was marvellous.

In a low, urgent, excited voice Henry Mastin said, "See that wench?"

Jeremy followed the direction of a jutted elbow. Approaching was a girl in her late twenties. She had a willowy body. Her face was attractive despite its paint. She kept touching a small hat as if, like the irrepressibly cheerful, its presence was a worry.

Going by, she exchanged nods with Mastin. He asked of Jeremy in a whisper, "Kick her out of bed?"

"No indeed."

"We have, shall we say, been friendly, that wench and I. Yes, *friendly*."

Rather coarse, Jeremy thought with fleeting discomfort and lingering jealousy. He would have liked to have not believed Mastin for a moment. But there was something about the way he had squared himself thoroughly.

"Pretty girl," Jeremy said. He stamped one foot.

"Yes."

"Recently?"

"Month or so ago," Mastin said. He fingered his paunch. "Well, must be getting back."

"So must I," Jeremy said dully. He added with an abruptness that surprised and perked him, "Of course, I don't *have* to hurry back."

"Oh no. I don't either."

"I set my own times. I wear the pants in my house."

"I do too. Honestly."

"I could stay out till all hours, if I wanted."

"So could I," Henry Mastin insisted. He asked, "How about another drink?"

They turned around.

※※※※※

An un-Edwardian, inelegant tune was being assassinated in a jukebox behind a curtain. No one in the crowd at the bar noticed. No fingers snapped, no toes tapped.

Henry Mastin said, on the heels of a shuddery sigh, "Just a slave in my house. That's what I am."

"Know what you mean," Jeremy said. His face was gaunt, his eyes were tragic. "I'm exactly the same."

Mastin shook his head waveringly. "Couldn't be, old man. Couldn't be. I'm the biggest slave I know."

"I'm under the thumb."

"Me, I'm a bloody doormat."

"Right under the thumb," Jeremy said. He demonstrated his meaning by pressing his hand into the spillage that surrounded the two full glasses of whisky.

Henry Mastin asked, "Know what Mona made me do?"

"No, old man. I certainly don't."

"I never told no bloody one about this."

"Well then."

Mastin cringed expectantly. "She made me give up cigarettes."

"Oh God," Jeremy said, obliging with a stare of horror and pity.

"Made me. Forced me. Said I was ruining the furniture. Said I was stinking the house out."

"Alice said the same. She made me stop smoking as well."

But that wasn't good enough, Jeremy felt. He needed something stronger to satisfy his craving to be confidential.

He played with confidences. He thought of saying he hadn't really streaked in Piccadilly Circus, but it wasn't fair to lie to his friend, his dear dear friend, his one and only mate.

"Washing up," Mastin said. "She makes me do it every night."

"Just a couple of servants, that's what we are."

"Walking the dog. Putting out the garbage cans. Going for shopping."

Henry Mastin lifted his glass with a slow, firm movement. Carefully, he poured whisky on his chin.

"Oops," Jeremy said. At once he forgot why he had said it.

"Thank you."

Jeremy leaned forward. He said, "Listen. I'll tell you this secret. Are you listening?"

"What?"

"My shoes are too big," Jeremy gasped, not far from sobbed.

"I know how it is."

"Far too big."

"Standing there at the sink with an apron on," Henry Mastin muttered. "It's soul-destroying."

"Too big altogether."

"And if it's not done just so. If there's any bits of food left on. Well."

"As big as could be," Jeremy said. He was wonderfully sad, as well as happy at his generosity.

"She'd like me to do the cooking too. I know. You can't tell me."

"Fit a bloody giant, my shoes."

"I've resisted so far. Fought a brave fight, I have. But I expect she'll win in the end."

Jeremy said, "These shoes—listen—these shoes are really *big*." His sorrow burst and he smiled.

Henry Mastin gave deep nods before saying, "Yes. Oh yes. She'll have me at it in the end, that Mona."

Jeremy's smile dwindled a twitch at a time. In blankness he said, "What?"

Mastin asked, "What you say?"

"Dunno. Cooking?"

"Washing shoes?"

Jeremy was feeling swirly. Turning away, he sprang his gaze

on a beer advertisement. It slid away sneakily. He chased it and caught it, watched it start to dance, became frightened, and turned back to Mastin, who asked:

"Cooking?"

"Alice is a good cook," Jeremy said. "I won't deny that."

"Okay."

"Well, she's not bad. Fair. Two stars." It seemed to Jeremy that he had pronounced the last word "shtars." He leaned forward to enunciate, "Shtars."

Henry Mastin said, "Mona cooks like . . . Mona cooks like . . . But anyway, look here. Now look here, old man."

"She makes me join things," Jeremy said.

"Who?"

"I join things."

"I have to do the washing up. Piles of it. Pots and pans. But look here."

Mastin took hold of his drink and raised it with elbow high. He got a good percentage of the alcohol in his mouth. Smiling crookedly at the glass, he put it down and wiped his hand across his soppy lips, fingers first.

Flinching like a barked-at dog, he gave Jeremy a hard look and said, "Steady on."

"She'll kill me for this."

"No violence."

"Kill me," Jeremy said. "Staying away till all hours of the night."

"Remember that song about three o'clock on a Sunday morning?"

"Slaughter me to pieces."

Mastin said, "Ah yes. Now I remember what I was going to say. Listen here, old man."

Jeremy looked at his glass. He felt nauseated. However, he thrust out his chin, lifted the glass, and said, "A man must have his freedom."

"That's it, Wood!" Mastin hissed, swinging forward. "That's exactly what I'm trying to say."

Jeremy put the glass down. "Quite."

"What it boils down to is this. A man must have his freedom. D'you see what I mean?"

"I do."

"And have we got freedom? Answer me that if you can. Have you got it, have I got it?"

Jeremy yawned. He was so unrestrained in this that his forearms trembled. He said, "No."

"That's exactly what I'm saying."

"Right. Spot on."

"Therefore, old man," Henry Mastin said, "we have to do something about it. And bloody soon." He leaned back and tried to fold his arms. They slithered loosely down his paunch like dead snakes.

"Yes," Jeremy said, intrigued by a passing attack of the swirls.

Henry Mastin, who seemed unaware of his head's loll, smiled with crafty eyes. "We need, in fact, to get the upper hand."

"I agree," Jeremy said. "I go along with you there."

"Thanks, old man."

"After all, a man must have his freedom."

"That's exactly what I'm trying to say. We need to get the upper hand, you see. And to get that, to get that, Wood, we need a lever."

This sounded familiar to Jeremy. Interested, he said, "Go on."

"A hold, you see. We need to get a hold over these tyrants. Once we've got that, we can tell 'em what to do with their old washing up."

Jeremy stayed his head. He asked, "How?"

Henry Mastin paused. He stared. Then, his face recovering, he nodded. "We'll have to make plans. Get organised. Have a conference."

"Okay."

"It won't be easy to bring off, mind you. But we'll do it. We'll have to."

"Or we're lost."

"Right. Lost to the world."

"We'll help each other," Jeremy said brightly. He pretended he didn't believe what his stomach told him—that he was going to vomit any second now.

Mastin grinned violently. "That's it, that's it. We'll all help each other. In fact, I'll help you and you help me."

"It's a deal," Jeremy said. "I'm going home."

He was outside. I am drunk, he thought gravely, proud of his truth. He felt that an important junction in his life had just been reached. He was at a milestone. The talk with Henry Mastin had been personally historic.

Jeremy stopped and, with an ungainly lurch, turned. As a gesture, an acknowledgement, an appreciation, he looked back at the place where it had all happened.

Mastin, sitting on the pub step, was taking off his shoes and socks. Jeremy nodded, turned, and strayed on.

A lever, he thought. A lever.

THREE

The Horsetrough Lane Residents Association was in closed session, the venue a house at the end of the street. Outside, three children with clean knees stood in offended attitudes and took turns at whispering insults through the letter slot.

Twenty-seven adults were crowded into a small front room. The majority sat in wedged proximity on stools, heels, the floor, and three to an armchair; or stood by the window avoiding one another's elbows.

At the room's farther end, fourteen feet six inches away, sat the Action Committee. The three people were in reasonable comfort at a card table, which twitched from time to time as its legs were kicked by crampy front sitters.

One of the Action Committee was reading out the minutes of the last meeting. An emaciated woman with doubting eyes, while speaking she supported her chin with a hand and kept its index finger straddling her lips.

The other hand clenched convulsively whenever the secretary, kneeling nearby, gave a dry laugh.

The other two Action Committee members, offended-looking older men, were straightening their ties and feeling their necks.

Res Ass, Jeremy thought in a brutal jibe, smiling with his lips pursed. Res Ass, Res Ass.

The minutes reader stumbled over a word. The secretary, a young woman with hair like spaniel ears, gasped and sprayed the gathering with looks of shock, like an auctioneer getting a good bid that might be bettered.

"It's perfectly clear," she hissed. "Quite quite clear."

Somebody shushed.

The secretary whispered, "Clear clear clear."

Fist staying clenched, eyes open again after a shuddered closure, the reader went on at a muffled, finger-split rant.

Res Ass, Jeremy thought.

He and Alice were sitting tailor-fashion near the front. Alice was rapt, Jeremy bored and resentful. He had succeeded in forgetting that he himself was to blame, that it was he who had insisted on coming here this evening. With satisfaction he embraced the conviction that attendance had been forced on him, as punishment. He was being made to play out an act of atonement.

Anyone would think, Jeremy told himself, that coming home just a teeny bit tiddly was the worst thing in the world. Alice's reaction had been monstrous. It was ridiculous, the way she had behaved ever since, going around saying absolutely nothing about it, always busily chattering of other matters. Not one solitary word had she said. Vicious. It was monstrous of her to make him feel so guilty.

Jeremy shuffled.

Leaning close, Alice whispered, "What's wrong? Uncomfortable?"

"I'm feeling guilty," he said, glaring like a gambler gone mad.

"What?"

He eased the glare. "Fifi. She ought to be having a walk."

Someone shushed. It was the same person as before, a short man with an aggressively mild appearance who never spoke at meetings. He only shushed.

"You can't leave now," Alice murmured.

"Poor old Fifers."

"I'd be mortified."

One of the Action Committee men said, "To business."

A voice from the back said, "And let's hope it's *real* business, Mr. Chairman. Not just words. What we need is the dynamic approach."

Another voice agreed: "We've had enough of shoes and ships and sealing wax, and cabbages and kings."

Looking around for the speaker, Jeremy, forgetting himself, said loudly, "I know the last line to that."

Alice pinched his thigh. He turned, blushing, and mumbled, "Well, I do."

"Mr. Chairman," the first voice said. "The time has come for the big leap forward. We need a large, new, visionary idea."

"You have a suggestion?"

"No."

Several other voices said together, "I have."

There was a rumble of movement as the speakers began to rise from the floor or move from their places at the back. Mr. Chairman told everyone to remain put. He was ignored.

Jeremy said sullenly, "Edward Lear." Alice shook her head.

Half the sitters were now in various stages of arising. They were disentangling legs, or fighting for balance, or slapping off the helping hands they thought were restraining. There was a faint shriek from a female. The shusher worked gamely.

"Isn't it exciting?" Alice whispered.

"Yes," Jeremy said. Calmly does it, he thought. He said, "I'm going."

"Oh."

"I can't stand the idea of poor Fifi missing her walk."

Alice's smile could have been translated as affectionate understanding. Jeremy chose to read in it: "I knew you'd wriggle out of this somehow."

"See you later."

He managed to gain his feet, to find islands of stepping places, to arm his way to the door, and to squeeze out.

Ten minutes later, after collecting Fifi from home, Jeremy was striding across Hampstead Heath. He felt buoyant and eager. Not one second did he waste on what would have been his normal pursuit, pretended worry of the invented-later Alice-trouble over his outwriggling. His eyes were searchingly on the way ahead.

When in the distance Jeremy saw Henry Mastin, he was satisfied.

The two men shook hands, smiled shyly, and found escape for their eyes in turning to watch their dogs, who were romping off together.

"Sorry I'm late," Jeremy said; this despite their having been no arranged rendezvous. Yet he felt as though there had, and Mastin evidently felt the same.

He said, "That's all right."

Jeremy loosened his tie. "I got hell for yesterday."

"Me too. It's been shocking."

Letting his face droop, Jeremy said, "You wouldn't believe what I've been through."

"I would," Henry Mastin said. "I know the score." He began to walk.

Jeremy fell into step at his side. He sensed the export of the situation, its outgoing consequence.

He said, "I've—er—been thinking."

"So have I."

"What we talked about."

"In the pub. Yes."

Jeremy sighed, smiling, and felt a prickle of excitement when Henry Mastin said, "I meant it."

"Good."

"I meant every single word, Wood."

"I did too."

"It's been on my mind ever since."

"Me too," Jeremy said.

"It wasn't the booze talking."

"Nor with me."

Mastin asked, "You remember exactly what we said?"

"Every word, old man."

Henry Mastin came to a halt. He turned to Jeremy and gave him a searching look. Jeremy made his face sincere.

"You agree that we must take matters into our own hands, do something about our predicament?"

"I do," Jeremy said. "We can't go on this way. It's asking too much of any man."

"Just so."

Jeremy said, "The time has come for the big leap forward."

"That's it, Wood."

"The dynamic approach, in fact."

"Now you're talking," Mastin said.

"It's no use going on and on about why the sea is boiling hot and whether pigs have wings."

"Er—no."

"Action."

"Yes," Henry Mastin said. "Concrete action. And I have an idea of what form that action should take."

"Ah?"

"Just an idea, of course. But it might work."

"You never know."

Mastin nodded. He moved away and began to stroll in a large circle around Jeremy. Clasping his hands behind, looking at the grass, he said:

"What we need, you see, is a lever."

"Precisely."

"I don't know if you'd thought of that."

Jeremy had thought of little else since the pub, except for Alice's not talking about him being tight. He said, turning slowly to keep Mastin in view, "Go on."

"Well, Wood, I think I know of a way to get that old lever."

"Good."

Mastin nodded at the grass as if it were a prompter. "Let's see what you think of this. It's only an idea, mind. But I think it's got something."

Jeremy added a nod of his own. His eagerness had given way to a steady expectancy.

"The ideal and classic solution," Mastin said, speaking as though after careful rehearsal, "is to discover that the woman in the case is having a love affair."

"Oh?"

"Yes. That sort of thing happens all the time. I mean the husband stumbling on the truth or being told it by a fourth person. Then he's got wifey just where he wants her."

"I suppose so," Jeremy said without enthusiasm.

"Of course, it's always accidental, his finding out, and accident is no good to us. I mean, is it?"

"Wait a bit," Jeremy said. "My wife isn't having an affair."

"No no no. Neither is mine. Not the type. No, what we've got to do, you see, is *create* a love affair. Two affairs. One for Mona and one for Alice. You see what I mean?"

"Not exactly."

"Listen," Mastin said, addressing the grass. "It's as plain as day. I have an affair with your wife, you have an affair with mine."

"Wouldn't work," Jeremy said, offended. "Though I do say it myself, Alice is a one-man woman."

"Oh, Mona is too. That's not the point. I didn't mean *really*. Not real love affairs. I meant *apparently*. See?"

Jeremy smiled, still turning in a slow circle to watch the other man. "Ah."

"Get me now?"

"Yes. It's good."

"Thank you," Mastin said, smirking. "It's not bad at all, is it?"

"Excellent."

"Yes, the idea's sound, I believe. Putting it into practise will be the problem."

"And the wife would deny the affair, naturally."

Henry Mastin said, "Unfortunately, the red-handed bit is out. You know, bursting into the bedroom."

"Yes, if they're not really at it, they can't be caught."

"True."

"Love letters," Jeremy said keenly. "We could do that ourselves, each on his own. I could write dozens of passionate letters to Alice, signed Bill or Jim or something. I'd make them real sizzlers. I'd put them in her wardrobe, tied with pink ribbon, and then pretend to find them."

Mastin shook his head. "She'd know at once it was a trick. She'd be on to you then, get your game. You'd be worse off than before."

Jeremy sank. "I suppose." He had been looking forward to writing those letters.

"We have a problem."

"A good one though," Jeremy said, brightening. "It's a challenge."

Henry Mastin stopped walking. He looked up. He and Jeremy grinned at each other.

"We're just a couple of old anarchists, Wood. That's what we are."

"Damn right, old man."

Mastin became businesslike again. "The red-handed thing," he said. "That's the way. Though let us stress *apparently*."

"Of course."

"If the husband walks in on the wife and another man and finds them in a compromising situation—you're home and dry."

"It needn't be too compromising, either."

"Which leaves the question of denial. The wife has to feel guilty even though she isn't."

"That's shrewd," Jeremy said.

Mastin smirked again. "There's some wild possibilities. For instance, the cuckolder says he's ripped his trousers and daren't go home. The wife tells him to take them off so she can mend them. He's just doing that when hubby comes in."

"*Or*," Jeremy said, "the cuckolder says he wants to show the wife a new dance step. He gets hold of her, moves her into position, pretends to trip, and falls with her onto the couch, himself on top."

"*Or*. He suddenly says he's got ants in his clothes and frantically begins to strip off."

"*Or*," Jeremy said, needled by his own pallid contribution. "*Or*." But he didn't go on. He couldn't think of anything else.

Thankfully, Mastin seemed to have reached the same block. He said, solemn, "But there wouldn't be any guilt, you see."

"No."

"There's got to be that."

Jeremy said, "A kiss would do the trick, you know. The cuckolder and the wife kissing. A friendly kiss. But it wouldn't look that way to hubby. And the wife would feel guilty."

"In fact," Mastin said forcefully, "the man could, at that moment, having set the procedure with friendly pecks so the wife is used to it, he could at that moment give her a genuine kiss. A real smackeroo. Eh?"

"Yes. I was just about to say the same thing." Jeremy felt calm. He knew the answer had been found.

"It might take weeks, months. And, of course, the timing would have to be perfect."

"And it might not work at all," Jeremy said. "But it would be interesting to work on. A fascinating project."

"Then that's the best plan?"

"If we go ahead, yes."

Henry Mastin tilted up his chin. His eyes were gleaming. "I'm game if you are, Wood."

"I'm game."

They stepped forward and shook hands. The grip was firm and final. They smiled, heaved sighs, and began to walk together.

"The first thing is introductions. The second is a sound reason to call when hubby is out."

"Excellent thought, that. We don't want to leave it to casual calls. That'd take too long to establish."

"We'll start with me," Jeremy said. "How do I get you well in with Alice?"

༄༄༄༄༄

"A constructive meeting," Alice told Mr. Barlow, who said, "Glad to hear it, me dear."

The trellisless neighbours were sitting on the Woods' patio. The table between them held cups, which had held tea.

Bald and beaky, crouched small inside his tweeds and Arran Island because Alice was wearing a trouser suit, Mr. Barlow asked:

"The next move?"

Happily and firmly, Alice said, "We're going to picket the Town Hall."

"That's the stuff."

"We're going to *show* them."

"Right!"

"Every banner," Alice said, snuggling forward over folded arms, "will have the same slogan."

"Which is?"

"Our Human Rights Are Being Trampled On."

"Phew!"

"Yes. Pretty strong stuff."

"Too strong, maybe?" Mr. Barlow's judicious lips extended themselves.

"Not at all," Alice said. "It's time we got tough."

"Perhaps you're right."

"We'll do the picketing later this week, as soon as the banners are ready."

"And his lordship?" Mr. Barlow asked.

He meant Jeremy. He always referred to him as that, or as "the man of the house," or "your lawful wedded," or "the good spouse," or "his nibs." Because "Mr. Wood" was too formal and "Jeremy" too familiar.

"Will his lordship join you on the picket?"

"Well," Alice said, drawing out the word as if it tasted nice, "I don't know."

"Why's that?"

"I haven't asked him yet. He might agree to join us though," Alice said. "He's getting quite adventurous lately."

"Oh?"

She grinned. "You'll never guess what he did last night."

The amateur dirty old man in Mr. Barlow was alerted. "Erm?" he encouraged.

Alice giggled. Mr. Barlow gasped.

"He's never done anything like it before."

"Yes yes, go on."

"Tipsy," Alice said. "He came home tipsy."

Mr. Barlow had the dreary suspicion that he had heard the punchline. Nevertheless he asked, "And then?"

"Well, I mean, that's it. He was *tight*. Jeremy, if you can believe it. He walked in like a zombie and went straight upstairs to bed. It was so funny. And I'm sure it did him a power of good. My father always maintains that a man should get sozzled every once in a while. He's been terribly sweet today. Jeremy."

Mr. Barlow grunted. He thought he was not having a very good evening this evening, what with trouser suits and everything.

Alice went on, "So you see what I mean about being adventurous. And he did go to the meeting tonight. I think he's coming out of his shell a bit."

"When I was his age," Mr. Barlow said.

"Yes?"

"Needs waking up, that lad."

Alice said, "So involved with his work, you see. Big plans. Ideas." She waved a hand. "You know."

"All work and no play," Mr. Barlow said. But he hadn't the heart to act. "I must be off."

Some minutes later, still warm with pleasure at her neighbour's parting compliment on the dress she had worn last week, Alice heard the front door open. She came out of the kitchen.

Jeremy, she was surprised to see, had not come home alone. There was a man with him. The stranger was portly and middle-aged and had hands that got in the way.

"Darling," Jeremy said, "this is Henry Mastin."

"Henry Mastin's the name," the man said, lurching forward to give a brisk handshake. "Delighted to meet you at last, Mrs. Wood."

"How do you do."

Jeremy said, "Mastin and I have known each other for ages. You've heard me mention his name, of course."

Alice nodded. She was convinced that Henry Mastin had been mentioned often. Living easily side by side with that, like neighbours in a coma, was a feeling of satisfaction that Jeremy had found a new friend.

"Known each other for simply ages," Jeremy said. "Haven't we, old man?"

"Yes indeed. Oh yes."

"A long time, in fact."

"Yes," Henry Mastin said, his hands furtively coming and going like brothel visitors.

Alice nodded again and wondered why she was nervous. "That's nice."

Gesturing with a low sweep as if laying a cloak, Jeremy said, "And this, dear, is Rover."

The dog lay in a panting slump by the door. Alice said, "Hello, Rover."

"He and our Fifi get along famously together. Don't they, old man?"

"They certainly do."

The three people stood smiling firmly at the sprawled dog. The seconds ticked by. Rover looked worried. Fifi, on her corner blanket, whined.

Alice was thinking of something to say. When she succeeded, she spoke simultaneously with the other two.

Alice: "How old is he?"
Jeremy: "Who's for a sherry?"
Mastin: "I'd better be running along."

After a pause, there came another confusion, one of voices and movement.

Nervous, Alice said "Yes" to her husband and "You mustn't think of it" to the guest. She and Jeremy set off together for sherry. Both turned back. Jeremy laughed strangely. Alice, distractedly, repeated her question: "How old is he?" Jeremy took Mastin by the arm and drew him toward the couch. Rover growled. Alice set off again for sherry. Mastin said, for the second time, that he would be forty-two next birthday.

Then there was peace. They were all sitting around the coffee table with full glasses. It occurred to Alice that perhaps it was not she herself who was nervous but the two men. Which thought she dismissed as foolish.

Henry Mastin said, "Nice place you've got here."

"Well, we like it," Jeremy said. "Cheers."

The glasses were drained, then refilled.

"This is pleasant," Alice said. She smiled fondly at her husband. She thought he was like a little boy who brings home a new playmate. One he has known for ages.

"The thing is this, Alice," Jeremy said, thumping forearms on knees. "This is the thing."

"Yes, dear?"

"Mastin and I met this evening, quite by accident. We're always running into each other like that."

The guest said, "Always."

"On the Heath, I mean, Alice. Never anywhere else. Not in town. Not in pubs and things."

Mastin said, "Oh no."

"So we met on the Heath, Alice, and as we strolled along, the subject of game came up. You know. Dominoes and stuff."

"Cards," Mastin said.

"Yes, cards, Alice. And I happened to mention that my wife was a bridge expert."

Alice blushed. "Really, dear. Hardly an expert."

Jeremy nodded at the guest. "First-class player."

"Well . . ." Alice said, still blushing happily. She looked at her glass.

Mastin said, "Then *I* mentioned that I've always wanted to learn how to play bridge. For years I've wanted to."

Jeremy: "And *I* said I could solve that little problem in no time flat."

Mastin: "And I asked how."

"And I said my wife will teach you."

Alice looked up. Both men were smiling, and watching her with fretful eyes. She said, feeling proud and powerful, "I don't know what to say."

Jeremy asked, "You could do it, give lessons?"

"Well, yes, I suppose so."

"Then there's no reason why you shouldn't give old Mastin a few. Or one, anyway, to see how it goes."

The guest organised his hands to support an invisible tray as he offered, "I might be no good at it."

Alice said, hinting at a lie, "Oh, anyone can learn bridge, Mr. Mastin."

"I'd be so grateful, Mrs. Wood. You've no idea how long I've wanted to learn."

"There you are, then," Jeremy said, jabbing aside with both elbows. "That's settled. Now all we need is to fix a date."

Eyes questioningly on the wall as she flipped through a mental engagement book, Alice talked of her Red Cross, her Society for Distressed German Ponies, her regular bridge, and her Horse-trough Lane Residents Association.

Jeremy snapped his fingers, then clapped his hands, then swung an arm, then leaned back with a heavy swoop. "Yes!" he cried.

Alice put a hand to her throat. "Yes?"

"Thursdays."

"Mmm?"

"Thursdays, darling. You know how you're always saying how lonely it is for you when I go to Bedford."

Alice couldn't remember saying that. Wondering why it was that her memory was so bad lately, she nodded.

"Well, that's the solution," Jeremy said. "This Thursday, Mastin can come along here for his first lesson."

Alice asked, "Will that be all right with you, Mr. Mastin?"

"Perfectly. Couldn't be better. It's very kind of you, Mrs. Wood."

"Not at all."

"Everything'll work out fine," Jeremy said. He winked broadly. "And you needn't worry about old Mastin, darling. He's quite respectable."

Everyone laughed.

Alice lifted her glass. She said, "You live in Hampstead, I take it, Mr. Mastin."

※※※※※

"You nearly chickened out," Jeremy said gleefully. He strode along Horsetrough Lane with a bounce.

"No such thing." Henry Mastin grinned, looking no less triumphant than did his companion.

"Oh yes."

"No no."

"You went for the door," Jeremy said, almost singing it out.

"'Course I did, old man. A crafty move, that."

"What?"

"Crafty. It got things moving, you see."

Jeremy smiled over an "Urm." He was not a man to be taken in so easily. Furthermore, he sincerely doubted now that Mastin had ever shouted in the Underground.

Which gave him a thought, which he chased by slipping mentally away into a duologue of the near future.

Jeremy: "That old Mastin's a funny bloke, Alice. He'll take anything as gospel."

Alice: "Yes?"

"Honestly. I told him I'd once streaked in Piccadilly Circus, and he *believed* me."

"Good heavens."

"I said you were there watching."

"Well I never."

"So if he should bring it up, don't spoil the story, eh?"

"I wouldn't dream of it, dear."

Relieved, Jeremy returned to the present. He graciously permitted Henry Mastin to talk about the value of crafty moves. His casual humming he kept to a low pitch.

"Presence of mind," Mastin said. "The old army training."

Quickly, afraid of an attack, Jeremy asked, "How far do we have to go?"

"Couple of streets from here."

"Let's step it out, old man."

"Keen for action, eh?"

"Yes," Jeremy said. "The fray's the thing."

He thought that rather good. He glanced at Mastin as they picked up speed. There was no response. Jeremy turned to call to the panting dog, "Come on, Poppy."

Soon they were walking through a gateway. Ahead burst a mammoth house, greystone Edwardian, timidly Gothic for the most part but with an occasional, hysterical hark-back in the form of gargoylian masonry.

The place would be silly by sunlight. It looked impressive now, with dusk edging in, and should have been removed at once to the jacket of a novel, with a threatened girl growing on the lawn.

"You live here?" Jeremy asked, unable to keep out of his voice that he was awed; and hurt.

"A bit of it. They made it into twenty-seven flats."

Strong again, Jeremy put a hand on Mastin's arm and brought him to a stop. "Listen, old man. Have you thought of anything yet?"

"Not a thing."

"Me neither."

"The old mind's a blank," Henry Mastin said. With docile face he stood looking at the house.

Jeremy suggested, "Photography. Stamps. Chess. Cycling."

"We've been through all those."

"There must be something."

"Must be."

"So we'll leave it as agreed," Jeremy said. "Just the introduction. Get that much settled at least."

"And you never know, something might come up in the conversation."

"Right."

They moved on, through double doors, across a hall, and up a staircase.

They stopped at a door and smiled weakly at each other. Henry Mastin got out a key and led the way inside. They were in a passage of gloom.

Lashed But Not Leashed

Rover loped on ahead. He went through a far doorway. From beyond there came a female voice giving a welcome and asking how was doze walkies den.

Mastin nodded off a confidence: "Mona."

"I see," Jeremy said. "Yes."

Mastin called, "Hello, love!"

The voice paused. When it started again, producing a single word, its warmth had gone. It said, "Evidently."

Jeremy whispered, "She's busy. I'll come another time."

Henry Mastin walked forward briskly. "I've brought a guest. Chap I've known for ages. Years. Asked him up for a drink."

He passed through the doorway. He stopped talking. There was silence.

Jeremy stood there. He sickened as the silence went on. He had a vivid picture of Mastin and wife making frantic signals at each other and mouthing words. Mastin's attitude was pleading; his wife's, outraged and demanding as she stabbed a signpost arm.

The situation being absurd to Jeremy, he suddenly saw the whole arrangement being so. The antiwife campaign was fantastic, ridiculous, vicious, hateful. It was the product of schoolboy minds. He would back out at once.

Jeremy turned to the door and fumbled at the handle. He felt as though he were in the credits of a nightmare.

Mastin called, "Come through, old man!"

"Thanks," Jeremy said, swinging around smartly. "Coming." His voice was lightly cracked.

Jeremy could not manage to bring off an elegant entrance. He tried an indolent smile; it looked like a simper. He tried a mild swagger; and hit his shoulder on the doorframe. He tried to control his hands; they somehow kept bumping together.

Coming to a stop, Jeremy forgot his smile and said a drastic, "Hello."

Mastin sliced about with his arms. "The little woman—Jeremy Wood. Wood—Mona."

"How do you do."

"How do you do."

Mona Mastin was a disappointment. Jeremy's surface mind had so strongly been expecting a fat ogress that subconsciously he had been confident he would see a sweet little beauty. Mona was neither.

She was tall, taller than her husband, taller than Jeremy. She had broad shoulders, a bosom area that was large but undefined as breasts, and ample hips, covered by a prickly sweater and navy-blue slacks with lint. Dark hair pinned back from a centre parting into a long ponytail.

Mona was handsome, in a stepmother way. Dark eyes, smooth tawny skin, a nose of thrusting consequence. The mid-thirties face had poise and serenity. In all, Mrs. Mastin was rather grand with a background hint of danger, like a knighted dentist.

Jeremy became aware that he and the others were talking weather. He made suitable comments. Next came the subject of drinks.

Mastin asked, "Is there still some of that Napoleon brandy left, love?"

Expressionless, his wife nodded. She said, "We'll have gin-tonics."

Henry Mastin turned on Jeremy a chaos of earnestness. "I love a gin and tonic."

"So do I."

Mona left the room. Mastin followed, after saying with loud heartiness, "Make yourself at home, old man."

Jeremy looked around. His nerves had settled, his hands were behaving. He thought only distantly of himself sometime putting an arm around those broad Mona shoulders and being looked at with an imperious, "What on *earth* are you doing?"

The room was small. Making it seem more so was an overlarge couch. In a velvet of pugnacious red, it swarmed in the centre position. There was little else. A fronting hearth, wall-hugging upright chairs, side tables: sycophants all.

Jeremy felt superior about the room. He smiled whimsically at its outdated wallpaper and chocolate-box prints. He found interest by looking in the mantel mirror and pulling a funny face. Next he stuck out his tongue. Last he bared his bottom teeth horrifically. That one he liked. He did it again.

Turning at sounds of approach in the hall, he brave-insanely held the horror face right until the last moment.

The hosts entered. Jeremy told himself fondly that he was just an old anarchist while saying a blithe, "Nice place you've got here."

Soon they were sitting, drinking, talking. Sidesaddle on a chair he had brought forward, facing his wife and Jeremy on the couch, Henry Mastin wheedled the conversation around to sports.

Mona gave a derisive snort. "Football. You're football mad."

"Oh, I wouldn't say that."

"Football mad. You wouldn't stay home on Saturday afternoons if the house burned down."

Mastin looked deep into his glass to say, "As a matter of fact. Yes, as a matter of fact. I'm going to a meeting of supporters on Thursday night."

"That's what I said. Football mad." She turned to Jeremy: "And you, Mr. Woods?"

"I'm not a soccer fan, no."

"There you are," Mona said flatly, as if Jeremy represented all males, as if her husband had been outvoted millions to one.

Mastin, still looking into his glass, said a sulky, "Well."

Mona began to talk about a keep-fit class she would like her husband to join.

Jeremy's nerves fretted like small saws chavelling plywood. He was worried about the conversation haing taken an unwanted direction. He decided to get it back on the right track. Gradually, cleverly like Mastin had done, he would work around to hobbies and things of that nature.

He said, "Hobbies."

Mona raised her thick eyebrows. "I beg your pardon?"

"Indoor games."

"Yes?"

Helplessly, shooting looks at Mastin, Jeremy hobbled on with, "I like them. You know. Games. Cards and things. Not that I know any. Oh no."

"It's important," Mona said, "to keep fit."

Jeremy nodded. "Poker. That's a good one. So I've heard. I'm mad keen to do something like that. There's nothing like a good indoor game or two."

Mona said, "If it were Henry who was chasing the football instead of watching, I wouldn't mind."

"Well," Mastin told his glass.

"My father was very fond of indoor games too," Jeremy said. "He takes after me. I'd rather go to an indoor game anytime than watch some silly old spectator sport."

Mastin sent him a vicious look.

"What I mean is," Jeremy said. "I mean."

Mastin turned his look on Mona, shuddered it into a flabby smile, and presented, "Football is as British as John Bull."

"That's a lot of bull," Mona said. She laughed briefly, a single clash of outgoing air that could almost be seen, like someone goosed in the cold.

Jeremy laughed with abandon.

Mr. and Mrs. Mastin watched him with calm interest. Humming off, he said, "Rich. Very rich."

"Oh yes," Mastin rushed. "It certainly was. Our Mona's quite witty. She comes out with some real snorkers."

Sober, Jeremy said, "Indoor games."

Mona Mastin rose. "I must get dinner moving. I'll leave you boys to your football talk. Good-bye, Mr. Wooden."

****

After the shop closed on Thursday, Jeremy put his overnight bag in the van and set off for Bedford. He drove mindlessly. Jeremy was not at his ease.

He kept thinking of his wife and Henry Mastin alone together. He was worried that they wouldn't get on, and afraid of them getting on too well. The latter notion he scoffed at. After all, there were the insurmountable barriers of Alice's devotion and Mastin's plainness. There were moments on the journey when Alice wore a nun's habit and Mastin needed plastic surgery. There were other moments, fewer but extant, when Alice-baby was accepting a lit cigarette from Henry-lover.

As for his own part in the creation of levers, Jeremy was upset by the lack of order in his campaign. Making the situation worse, like treacle in honey, was Mona's sophistication and cool.

It had been decided the evening before, during a walk on the Heath, that Jeremy would go to the Mastin flat on Saturday afternoon. He would ask for Henry, pretending he had forgotten about football. Presumably, Mona would invite him in; they would chat and perhaps have tea; a precedent might be set. In Jeremy's view, it was all most unsatisfactory.

He was not, therefore, at his ease. Each time he glanced at trees and murmured, "Simba," he was brought back by nervous excitement before he could get even a foot in the flora.

When Jeremy arrived in Bedford, the factory was closed and silent. He changed, ignored the paperwork, locked up, and went out to walk.

He strode quickly, head down and hands clasped behind, face set.

Jeremy had recalled for cruel duty the time on the pub step when Mastin had said of a passing woman, "We've been *friendly.*"

Jeremy wrestled with possibilities while chewing his lip.

The man could be a skilled seducer. Could, in fact, be a seducer who with evil brilliance went about his job helped, unknowingly, by the husbands. See, he could meet them on the Heath or in town, get friendly, get talking, maybe have a few drinks, and then propose an exchange of traps for the bossy wives.

Mastin could have three or four of these deals going at the same time, each in a different stage of development—the getting friendly, the drinks, the introduction. He might be a master of disguise. He might have been doing this for years. And, the thing is, he could have a special technique for seduction, hypnotism or drugs or whatever, so that the most faithful of wives wouldn't be able to resist. Once he's got entree via the poor innocent trusting husband—well. There you are.

Jeremy invoked a picture of Alice, naked, lying on their bed. She was spread-eagled and had glazed eyes and was being toyed with at leisure by Henry Mastin.

Jeremy stared at the picture. He was aghast. He was also vaguely titillated, which worried him.

As a break between bouts, he went into a snack bar, where, drooping, he drudged through a sandwich and ignored another man at the counter who tried to make conversation.

Afterwards, he continued his walk and his fret. It was midnight when he got back to the factory. Exhausted in mind and body, he fell asleep immediately. He was still dreaming of glazed eyes when the first employee arrived.

Jeremy spent the morning being sharp with his manager and going over the paperwork left the previous night. Not only did he fail to notice the secretary, Miss Cox, he left for home before their usual eleven-o'clock coffee break.

Ten miles outside Bedford, Jeremy stopped at a café to use the telephone. He called Henry Mastin at his office. Jeremy was relieved by the other man's breezy manner.

"Good morning, Wood old man. Lovely day."

"What," Jeremy asked, "about last night?"

"Worked like a charm. Nothing to it. I was there for two hours."

"Any. Er. You know. Um. Progress?"

"Progress? Yes indeed. I should jolly well think so."

"Oh?" Jeremy said grindingly.

"In fact, old man, we got on first-name terms."

"Ah."

"Alice and Henry, that's us. Nothing to it. Actually though, I'm quite proud of myself."

Jeremy decided he could forget his fear. He did so. The vague titillation of the night before became a vague disappointment.

He asked, "Next Thursday?"

"Yes, we settled that. I'll be there again for another lesson."

"Well, that leaves me and Mona."

Mastin said, "I have an idea for your side of this, as a matter of fact."

"I need one."

"Come now, old man. It's not that bad. One just uses one's initiative."

Jeremy's nerves crinkled at Mastin's tone of superiority. It's all right for you, he thought. Where would you have bloody been without bridge?

He said, "I suppose so."

"Anyway, when you call there on Saturday—tomorrow—it might be an idea to mention Stella Moorfield."

"A friend?"

"A novelist. Very famous. Writes historical romances. They're so pure they're awful. But old Mona, she's mad about Moorfield."

"I see."

"Mention her name, sort of casually, and you'll've made a friend for life. Stella Moorfield. Now you can't go wrong."

"No."

Mastin said, "Not getting cold feet, are you?"

"Oh no," Jeremy said. "I'll be there tomorrow."

****

It was two o'clock. Overcast skies increased the silence of the afternoon. Jeremy paused at the gate to straighten his tie. He wondered if he should squeeze the knot down to microscopic, a la Mastin. It might get him off on the right toe with Mona. But she could be sick to death of small knots. Also, he might never get it undone again. He might spend the rest of his life wandering around with . . .

Jeremy went on, moving his tie.

He was nervous. He felt like a job applicant with bad breath. He felt like an earl about to propose to a miner's daughter. He felt like going home.

What kept Jeremy was the look of scorn he would undoubtedly get from Mastin should he falter.

Jeremy had spent the previous evening in the Hampstead Public Library. He had leafed through a dozen Moorfield titles, getting gists. Additionally, he had learned from a reference book that the author was Percival Osbry-Wayn, who wrote under one other alias and listed his hobbies as flower arranging, wine, and embroidery. Jeremy was armed and ready.

His tie back in its original place, he went on. Inside the house, he climbed slowly. He experienced a growing nausea, like the running-down thrill after seeing an accident.

The door. Yes, this was the door. He knocked; and his heart seemed to be performing an echo. Hearing sounds of life from inside the flat, he winced.

He took a step back as the door opened.

Mona Mastin stood there tall and strong. She growled. Jeremy had not quite started on being astonished by the growl when he realised that it had come from Rover, glimpsing the dog behind Mona's legs.

"Well, hello," he said sloppily. He flickered a smile.

Her face was expressionless. "Hello."

"I thought I'd call in and see Henry," Jeremy said. "I just happened to be passing. You know."

"Yes?"

"You know. Walking past. On my way home. I was on my way home from the library."

"Henry's out."

"Ah."

"Football."

"Of course," he said. "Silly of me. Forgetting."

Mona said, "Come in." She commanded Rover, "Go to your basket."

Jeremy stepped inside and closed the door. Abruptly, the atmosphere was different. It had changed radically. It was like switching your head from one vista to another. Jeremy was dizzy.

He and Mona were standing close together in the hall's dimness. Their breathing was the only sound. Like the product of a B studio, Mona's features were not distinctive. Jeremy would not have been able to put into words what it was that had changed from one minute ago. It was everything.

Mona spoke. Her voice was low. She asked, "You hadn't really forgotten about the football, had you?"

Jeremy whispered, "No."

"I knew it."

Jeremy's dizziness had gone. His mind was clear but numb, as if in need of sleep. At the same time, his nerves were still jittering like animal fur in the wind. He was wondering how Mrs. Mastin had discovered his interest in Stella Moorfield. Or rather, he was telling himself that this was what he was wondering.

Mona swayed, moving closer. Her bolster of a bosom touched Jeremy's chest. She looked down at him and said, "I knew you'd come back."

"Really?"

"I wasn't sure when, but I knew you'd come back sooner or later. Alone."

"Yes."

They were both whispering.

"Shall I call you Jeremy?"

"All right . . . Mona."

"I knew because of the way you acted the other night. You couldn't keep your eyes off me. I could feel you looking at me the whole time."

"Ah. Yes. Well."

"And you kept on about indoor games. You kept on and on about them."

"That's true," Jeremy said slowly. He was hypnotised by the quiet voice and the steady gaze into his left eye. The matter of the words he was still patting into shape, though hesitantly.

Mona whispered, "I was surprised Henry didn't suspect. I mean, you kept on and on. It was so obvious what you were getting at."

"It was?"

"Oh yes. I understood all right. But not Henry. He's a bit slow at times. Luckily."

Jeremy thought it wouldn't be polite to agree—about the slowness. He murmured, "Mmm."

Mona shifted her gaze down to his mouth. "Mmm," she copied, lips pouting.

Jeremy smiled at her little joke. He told himself he was glad she had a sense of humour.

Mona said, "*You're* not slow, Jeremy."

"Oh no," he said. He laughed. He didn't know why.

"Nervous?"

"Well . . ."

"I am as well. Let's have a little drinky."

"All right."

She turned and went along the hall. Jeremy followed. He smiled to counter the naughty idea he was beginning to get. It was only an inkling, newborn and quite ridiculous; it just went to show how innocent phrases could be mininterpreted.

He went on smiling glaringly as, complying with Mona's suggestion, he went alone into the living room and made himself at home. He sat on the red couch.

His cheeks were starting to ache by the time Mona came in with two glasses. She gave him one, went to the window, and drew the curtains.

"Cozier," she said.

Relaxing his face in the gloom, Jeremy agreed: "It is, yes."

Mona returned to the couch and sat at his side. "More intimate."

"Yes."

"Here's cheers."

"Cheers."

Jeremy sipped. The drink was brandy, neat. He went on sipping because he didn't know what else to do. When the glass was empty it was taken from him by Mona, who turned away to put it and her own on the floor.

She turned back. She came touch-close to Jeremy and slid her arm along the seat behind him. He tried that smile again. It trickled away.

Looking straight ahead, knees primly together and pretending not to notice the pressure of one of Mona's, Jeremy said creakingly, "Stars in the Morning Sky." It was a Moorfield title.

"Poetry," Mona whispered. "I love it."

Her arm went to his shoulders, her head zoomed in, and she put her tongue in his ear.

He was stunned. Unaware that his hands had unclasped and that one arm was snaking through to encircle Mona's waist, he gaped ahead and thought:

Well well. Good heavens. My goodness. Jesus Christ. Well well well.

Jeremy's eyes shot down to their lower extreme limit as he saw Mona raise a hand. It unfastened the buttons of her blouse, went inside, fumbled and jerked, then retreated quickly.

Goodness gracious me. This isn't true. Oh no. Not at all.

He brought up his hand anyway. Dreamily, he watched it.

Jeremy's sensuality increased. His eyes started to ache from the hungry downcast stare, so he took turns in closing one eye and then the other.

He trembled with fear and excitement. He was hardly conscious anymore of his drooling ear.

Now Mona left it. She put a hand to his head and pulled it around. His neck gave three cracks. Mona kissed him swarmingly on the mouth. He could taste wax.

He kissed back manfully.

Jeremy became progressively more stunned, even as his desire continued to grow. He no longer had detached thoughts about the situation. He was living it entirely, not standing back in part to view.

A pip of a squeak erupted from deep in his throat as he felt Mona grip his thigh. Kissing absently, like a politician looking at the baby's mother, he tuned to the progress of the hand as it began to climb.

Mona slid her mouth away from the kiss and looked down. She said a lowing, "Oooh."

Jeremy hurt his throat with a cross between a gasp and a giggle.

Despite the fact that his neck ached, Jeremy pulled her back to the kiss. His desire was ranting and stamping and giving coarse laughs.

He reached for Mona's knees. At his touch they moved apart.

Jeremy forged on. He was overcome by a feeling of tranquility. His body relaxed and his mind switched to happy lethargy. It was as if he, the imminent riser, had been told that he could sleep for another hour.

He was not left in peace for long.

"I'm ready," Mona said with a gasp.

It was like a bell to signal the start of a wrestling match. Jeremy was at once involved in violent movement. He was lifted, bumped, twisted. He seemed to be on the way to victory, for he had the superior position, but he was in a crushing limb-grip.

A pause came while a clever and hasty hand seeped between their bodies to aim him in the right direction.

Gritting his teeth, Jeremy attacked. The arm of the couch was a gift; his feet used it for leverage.

Jeremy's mind was split three ways. He was concerned with his urge to come to a successful end; he was afraid of falling to the floor; he had the dread that his shoes might fly off.

Mona began to gurgle.

All Jeremy's worries ceased as he felt his desire run screaming to a crescendo.

Peace again.

Jeremy mumbled dreamily. His feet snuggled together against the couch arm like fed kittens.

Presently, Mona said, "Mmph."

He and Mona cleared their throats. He stood, turned his back, and made his person seemly.

Mona loomed up close beside him. Her clothing had been corrected. Since their faces were level, Jeremy assumed that Mona was sagging at the knees.

She said, "Divine."

"Marvellous."

"The divine Jeremy."

"The gorgeous Mona," he chanted, simultaneously forgiving himself.

"Another little drinky?"

"As a matter of fact," Jeremy said, looking at his watch without seeing it, "I haven't the time."

"You must away?"

"Business."

"What a shame."

"Yes," he said. He was beginning to feel trapped. He wanted to get out of this dream.

"But you'll come again?" Mona asked. She repeated her question, simpering the verb.

Nodding, Jeremy circled the couch and moved to the door. Mona followed, therein growing several inches. She said:

"This is pure folly, of course. I don't know what possessed us. But we must meet again."

"All right."

"It's fated."

"Yes."

"Monday afternoon? He's at work every day."

"Well, I am too," Jeremy said. He was at the front door now. "It's not going to be easy."

"But you, Jeremy, you're your own man. You're the boss. You can get off whenever you like."

"I'm terribly busy just now. We're having a sale. Perhaps not until next Saturday."

"Thursday evening. He's going to another supporters' meeting."

Jeremy said, "I'll be away in Bedford." He opened the door. "Saturday."

Lashed But Not Leashed 67

Tall Mona swayed close. Jeremy slipped out and moved off with a hissed, "Farewell."

A minute later he was outside, walking away and gaping about him stupidly.

FOUR

On Monday afternoon, Alice Wood was shopping in the High Street. Alice was a picture. Pausing or walking, she was a vision of vitality, of prettiness and happiness and health.

She felt that way. Today particularly. For Alice, the beginning of something was always good, be it a week or a party or whatever. Endings were sometimes sad, sometimes dreary. Beginnings were always fine. Early morning was lovely.

And of course, Alice thought as she tripped along the High, the weekend had been special, a tonic. All due to Jeremy. He had been quite, quite different. Not that he was ever dull. Oh no, not in the least. But for the past couple of days he had been cheerful and attentive, more like a boyfriend than a husband. Business must have improved.

A frown took a brief fling across Alice's face. She felt uncomfortable about imputing Jeremy's weekend manner to commerce, indeed to any outside influence. Why couldn't it be simply that he was happy?

Seeking escape from her discomfort, Alice darted into a shop. Fortuitously, it was a confectioner's. She ordered gaspingly, and paid for in fumbles, a cream cake of the gooey kind that Jeremy coveted.

Outside again, cleansed, Alice went back to thinking about the weekend.

Saturday they'd had an early supper, more of a high tea really, followed by an unscheduled visit to the movies. Marx Brothers, thousands of years old and an absolute scream. You didn't get funny pictures like that anymore; nowadays it was all sex, and people jumping on each other's heads, and having babies and things. After that they walked up to Jack Straw's Castle for champagne cocktails. Three each! My word. It had been quite an effort to get home without falling asleep.

Sunday morning, Alice mused preeningly. On Sunday morning. Hadn't that been nice? It was such a lovely feeling, posh, to be brought a cup of tea in bed and ordered to stay there until called down for breakfast, which Jeremy did so nicely, table set just so, mitred napkin, flower in a vase. Everything had been perfect. It had been intriguing as well, that singed flavour of the eggs.

And then a lazy, slouchy read of the newspapers, with Jeremy waxing brilliant on what awful rubbish they put in the scandal sheet on Sundays, a good half of which couldn't be true, they made it up, all those affairs and orgies and secret couplings going on was impossible, people weren't like that. Afterwards he took Fifi for a long, long walk.

In the afternoon, without having to be coaxed or even asked, Jeremy went with her to the Town Hall. While everyone picketed with Our Human Rights Are Being Trampled On, he watched staunchly from across the street. The outing was an unqualified success as far as the Horsetrough Lane Residents Association was concerned. Of course, as someone pointed out, it would have been slightly better if the Town Hall hadn't been closed. But Sunday was the only day they could all get together, and anyway several people did stop to ask what was going on. So there you are. Success.

An edge of defiance in her bounce, Alice went on her way. She had recovered from the success of the picketing by the time she had bought two steaks and a pound of sausages. She turned into a supermarket.

Leaving her bag on a hook by the door, Alice set off with a cart. She sometimes pretended she was driving a car, an ability she lacked, and enjoyed mental criticism of the aisle-hoggers and wild overtakers.

Once upon a recent time, Alice had taken driving lessons. The first day, showing that she was no stranger to a car, she had opened the door masterfully into the instructor's face. Day two, confused by orders, she had made a signal inside instead of out and slapped him in the same place. Turning to ask a question on the third day (the instructor now sitting behind), she had run up the kerb and frightened an old woman. The fourth day, parked outside the garage, she learned to switch all the lights on, and off. The fifth day she was told by the instructor that a new law demanded a firm cut-down on clients; she would get her money back, plus a bonus; she said she would put her name down for next year, and as they parted the man had tears in his eyes.

At a safe speed, Alice browsed around the supermarket. She drew into the side to pluck her choices and glanced behind before pulling out.

Distraction came in the form of a carted child. Alice made baby noises, refused to see the snotty nose, grinned at the cheerless mother, and thought: One of these days.

Which brought to her mind last night.

Her neck flushing, Alice shot away. She crashed into another cart and tangled wheels. Even though fully convinced that she was in the right, she apologised to the other person, a man in overalls who kept showing the whites of his eyes as he looked at the ceiling. It was obvious, Alice thought, that he had been drinking.

Moving off, she returned to her dwell on bed.

Jeremy had been marvellous. The casual observer would never have guessed that they'd been married for years and years. Just like honeymooners, though better, because there was no awkwardness and no worry about if you were doing it right. Lovely. A perfect climax to the weekend.

Giggling at the joke, which she decided was wit and not accident, Alice cornered neatly and pulled into the side by the pasta stand. As always, she was cowed by the selection. She began to finger her top lip.

She noticed a clock. It told her she was late. She shot off for the check-out, recklessly not pausing at a major cross-aisles.

When Alice got home, Jeremy had just arrived from work. Like new friends, they greeted each other with eager affection. Fifi ran madly around the room.

Jeremy rubbed his hands together. "How about a little drinky? Um, how about a gin and tonic?"

"Now? Before you've changed?"

"Certainly. We're not tied by routine, after all."

"You're right, dear. You're so right."

Soon they were sitting on the couch, sipping drinks. Alice told of her day.

Jeremy talked of doings at the shop. Alice was pleased to hear that business was not particularly good.

Drinks finished, Alice said, "I must put the steaks on."

Jeremy moved closer. "No hurry, love." He put his arm around her. "Let's neck for a while."

Alice sparkled pinkly. "Oh . . . well . . ."

He kissed her on the lips. She responded happily. Their embrace tightened. The kiss lingered and heated and took on depth. They sank back low on the couch.

Alice was mildly shocked. There was a time and a place for such things, after all.

"After last night?" she asked.

"Love," Jeremy said. "Just because we're married, that's no reason for romance to die."

Alice answered quickly, "Oh no. Not at all. How silly I am."

"I'm not in my grave yet." There was a pout in his voice.

They embraced and kissed. Their kiss became gossipy, all tongues.

Alice was growing interested. Sensuality had banished embarrassment and flattery had chased shock.

Glimpsing a movement from the corner of her eye—she opened it to see if Jeremy had his eyes closed—she drew back to look. Jeremy also turned.

Through the french windows they saw Mr. Barlow. He was setting up a deck chair on his patio.

"Oh dear," Alice said.

Sitting straight, Jeremy said, "And we can't very well pull the curtains."

"Oh no. Not now."

"Never mind."

She patted his hand. "Later, dear."

He winked. "Later, wife."

They smiled at each other, Jeremy with heavy eyelids like those of a tired camel. Alice drew back her pink sparkle.

"Steaks," she said, getting up in a flounce.

In the kitchen, working, Alice felt a retrospective excitement. She also felt ashamed of the nasty anti-Barlow thought that had come when she had seen him.

Dinner set to cooking, Alice went outside via the kitchen door. She moved to the wall, lifted her foot onto it, and said, "Good evening, Mr. Barlow."

~~~~~~

Upstairs, Jeremy whistled stridently as he changed from his work clothes. Now, out of Alice's presence, he felt bold and strong, a new man. He had been that way ever since his successful seduction of Mona. Thoughts of that masterly conquest had afterwards filled him with pride.

It was only when he was with Alice that Jeremy's new man became an old weakling. The pride turned to guilt, more a stuffing than a filling.

It had been a nerve-nattering weekend of ups and downs, of whale-dung lows and cloud-eating soars. The best moment had been his victory strut away from the Mastin flat, once his shock had receded. His worst moment, later that Saturday, came when, evilly, he had been obliged to press champagne cocktails on Alice to forestall with sleepiness the possibility of sex.

Jeremy whistled. He held one eyebrow in a blasé tilt while he knotted his tie in the mirror. He knotted it largely.

Sitting on the bed, he put on his six socks; the two rolls he kept hidden in the toes of slippers he never used. That done, he reached for the waiting shoes. He paused, looked, and withdrew the hand. His mood changed.

New Jeremy found the continuing existence of the shoes infuriating. He felt slighted, like a bested magician.

Jeremy stared down thoughtfully at the brogues, which had at least placed themselves in a pigeon-toed attitude of humility.

His mind shovelled into the mound of gambits. The old ones were gently set aside. Straining, digging hard, he at last brought up one that was steamingly fresh.

His eyes misted, his vision blurred, he did a slow fade to a flashforward scene in the living room.

"Those shoes I bought recently, Alice."

"Yes, dear?"

"You won't believe this, Alice. I can hardly believe it myself. In fact, it would be quite funny if it weren't so damned annoying."

"What is it, darling?"

"The shoes. They've *stretched*."

"No!"

"Yes, Alice. Stretched. I was out in the rain yesterday. It might not have rained here, but it did around the shop. It poured down. Torrents. The shoes got soaked."

"Yes, they would do that, naturally."

"And this morning I discovered they'd stretched."

"Well I never."

"I shall take them back, Alice. I'll probably be quite nasty about it."

"Not without reason, dear."

After the fade-out, Jeremy's plump grin of satisfaction snapped to a smile of triumph. He had found the *real* answer. It had come to him suddenly out of his new strength.

He put on the shoes, whose hash, he waggishly and smirkily assured himself, he would very soon settle. He left the room and went downstairs.

At the whatnot shelf he checked over his mail. There was nothing of interest. He flipped through *Punch,* smiled at the cartoons, and didn't think to look at his ad at the back.

Doffing a yawn of sophistication, Jeremy circled the couch and sat on it in a casual sprawl. He looked through the french windows. Slowly, his features sagged, his ebullience seeped away: he was back in the presence of Alice.

Making him feel worse was that she looked so girlish and dear, standing there with one leg up, foot on the wall. And she was being so kind to the lonely Mr. Barlow, who appeared forlorn, sunk low in the deck chair with the bottom half of his face hidden in the neck of his sweater. He might even be dead if it weren't for the fact of both hands shading his eyes and the rapid tapping together of his toes.

As Jeremy's mortification increased, he sat up straight, his face greying like the stone of a distinguished temple. He told himself he had been insane to let that woman have her way with him.

How could he have been so weak? Mona might, of course, have slipped something into the whisky before bringing it in from the kitchen. A narcotic or an aphrodisiac. Either that or he had been taken by a passing madness. Well, that was the end. Never again.

Jeremy decided to call off at once the whole scheme. He would not see Mona again, nor would Henry Mastin come here on Thursday. The plan had been absurd in the first place.

Getting up swiftly, Jeremy rounded the couch and went toward the telephone. At which point he remembered that he and Mastin had agreed never to call each other at home, only at work. Jeremy had, indeed, telephoned Mastin that morning at his office to report on the Saturday visit to Mona. A friendly chat, he had said. Quite nice.

"That's odd, Wood. She didn't mention that you called."

"Really?"

Mastin asked in a suspicious tone, "Are you sure you did?"

"Absolutely. We talked about books. It was nice and bright there, the sun coming in the uncurtained windows and everything, and me sitting on a stool by—"

"Then why," Mastin sliced in, "didn't she tell me?"

"I don't know."

"I gave her the opportunity. I asked if she'd seen anyone."

Jeremy said, "Perhaps she's afraid you'll be jealous."

"Not Mona."

"Anyway, I did call."

"Mm."

"Will you be over at my place Thursday?"

"I suppose so. Yes. I'm going to keep *my* end of the deal."

"So am I."

Mistrust had been as thick in the air as cockney scurf.

Jeremy thought now that all he need do was ring Mastin tomorrow and tell a lie—admit he had not gone to the flat. That would resolve the matter. The scheme would die.

Calling to Fifi, Jeremy went out into the street.

On the other hand, he thought, being considered a coward by Mastin was a bit hard to take, nor was it pleasant to know that he had backed out of a bargain. They had shaken hands on it.

Mona didn't tell him, Jeremy mused crowingly. She's head over heels. Completely smitten.

He swaggered, caught sight of Fifi bounding ahead, and thought: But it has to finish. So, the thing to do is arrange for Mastin to come home next Saturday and find us in a compromising situation. Nothing too strong. An arm around the waist—something like that.

However, Jeremy mused, unawarely tilting his head to one side, next week might seem too quick. Wouldn't want old Mastin to think anything had really developed between them. Wouldn't want to hurt the poor sod. Decent enough bloke. Suffered for years under the thumb. Washing dishes. Walking dogs. All that. So, no twist of the knife. Better to make it the Saturday after next.

Jeremy was pleased with the arrangement. He went on feeling pleased, and virtuous, as he agreed with himself that on this coming Saturday he would stay with Mona only ten minutes, and be quite firm with her if she came on strong.

※※※※※※

Thursday morning, Jeremy went to a shop near his own. He smiled politely but with total rejection at the girl assistant who came toward him craning a grimace of enquiry over clasped hands. A male clerk lounging by the counter was his goal.

Stopping beside the man, Jeremy said, brisk as a bus conductor, stabbing downward with a forefinger:

"I'd like a pair of shoes exactly like these, if you please. Only two sizes smaller."

"Oh?"

"You have this model in stock?"

"Well, yes."

"Good," Jeremy said. "I'll take them with me."

Nodding, the clerk moved away. He walked in a manner that Jeremy told himself was crestfallen. It made up for the fact that there had not been the expected argument, the one Jeremy had visualised several times and in which he had been thunderously victorious, after scoring point upon sarcastic point.

Boxed and wrapped and tied, the shoes were handed over. After receiving his change, Jeremy delivered the coup de grace:

he gave the clerk a tip. Turning away with a snatch of hum, he strode out.

He stopped briefly in another shop to buy a pair of socks, the thinnest of nylon. The woman gave him no trouble whatever. Nothing to it, he thought, buying clothes.

At Wood's Rustic Furniture he went into the lavatory to change into his purchases. The new shoes were snug. He felt supported and sure-of-foot.

For five minutes he worked at removing the look of newness. He scuffed at the uppers with the lavatory brush, and scraped a coin on the welts. Satisfied—proud, even—he put his old shoes and their six socks in the box, which he locked securely in his desk.

He strolled up the shop, to where large-headed Mrs. Hendon was putting price labels on peeled three-leggeds. He gave his throat an acute clearing. Mrs. Hendon turned with a start, her face twitching.

"Sorry," Jeremy said loudly, as though he were refusing in pale indignation to do someone a favour.

Mrs. Hendon also said, "Sorry." Her manner was one of cowed apology.

"Did I startle you?"

She nodded. Jeremy did not, as was customary when Mrs. Hendon performed a nod, sink into a hint of a crouch with hands out ready to catch. He simply said, "Ah."

"I didn't hear you coming, Mr. Wood, that's all. Sorry."

"Sorry."

"It's better when you've got your corduroys on."

It occurred to Jeremy that Mrs. Hendon had been less brisk of late, these past few days. But she was, after all, getting on.

"Yes," he said. "Seems a waste of energy though, changing clothes at Bedford. No?"

"I suppose so, Mr. Wood. I mean, certainly. Quite."

Jeremy jacked his chin and sent his shoulders square. In a brutally jovial tone he said, "Well, carry on, Mrs. Hendon. Don't let me disturb you. Do carry on."

"Yes, Mr. Wood. Thank you. Sorry."

Hands clasped aft in jiggling comfort, Jeremy strolled tight-footedly back to the rear and through a door. There was a moment, brief and at once forgotten, when he worried lest his head hit the top of the doorframe.

Tom Barr, kneeling by a chair, was in the middle of a wet coughing fit. From his slitted mouth and the cigarette it held came a spray of spittle, ash, and sparks.

"Tom," Jeremy said reprovingly. He adopted a headmaster pose, arms forward and one foot forward. "Tom, Tom, Tom."

The driver/handyman looked up squalidly. Wincing, he swiped back his greasy hair, using rough affection as if it were on the head of a young brother. He spat out the cigarette, pivoted his toe on it, and said:

"I know, sir. I know I shouldn't. It's dangerous. All this wood around."

Which is not what Jeremy had meant. But he switched to believing it out of shock: he had never heard Tom Barr say so much, ramble on at such length.

"Highly dangerous."

"Yes, sir. I forgot, like. I was wrapping these legs and just forgot. Wrapping away I was. Lost in it."

"You find your work interesting?" Jeremy asked, showing his Adam's-apple. He felt languid, the way he would if he were buying a second yacht.

"Oh yes, sir. Very. Oh very."

"Good."

"It's, well, it's"—fighting for words, waving the roll of paper and the adhesive tape—"it's *interesting*."

"I'm glad to hear that, Tom."

"Yes."

"Well, do carry on. Don't let me disturb you." Jeremy had liked the ring of this earlier. "Do carry on."

"Yes, Mr. Wood, sir."

Jeremy returned to the shop. The morning passed as pleasantly as an enemy's hearse. He answered letters in dashing terms, and left none for Mrs. Hendon. He stood out front with fingers tapping on his chest and thumbs that ached for suspenders. He cast many a facetious glance at the drawer that held his shoes.

At lunchtime Jeremy went to the local pub. Snacking, sipping lager, he chatted autocratically down to an appreciative, wincing barmaid. She looked the kind of woman who should be beaten regularly, like retreats by a coward.

The rest of the day Jeremy spent wandering around the shop and being a quiet nuisance. Three potential sales he spoiled by hovering with an amused expression. Once Mrs. Hendon asked him, timidly, when he was leaving for Bedford.

"Soon," he said, strolling off.

Jeremy realised he was not, as usual, eager to get away. He put this down to the boredom of routine, while factually what held him was reluctance to leave the locale of his sexual triumph, which, he believed in a dark, unexplored closet of his mind, was known about by many mysterious others, people who looked at him with respect and nudged the ignorant.

Jeremy was like a boxer who, after his bout, can't bear to leave the stadium and the limelight; who haunts the aisles, grip in hand, unnecessary sticking plaster prominent.

He locked up the shop himself. In a suburb near Hampstead, looking about him slyly (though unconscious of the act), he parked and went into a pub and had a leisurely meal.

Satiated, he left and drove on.

The sky was black with glints of bright, like a storm of magpies. The other cars were companionable and knowing. Jeremy told himself he should drive by night more often. Only once did he wonder, cheerily, how Mastin and Alice were getting on with their bridge.

It was late when he arrived. He went straight to his cot. His sleep was as deep and untroubled as that of a hypochondriac with insomnia.

The next morning, the employee whom Jeremy noticed most was Miss Cox. It was because while at her desk she kept calling for his advice, while moving kept getting in his way, and while standing kept giving shrill laughs.

She looked different. In addition to more cosmetics, her hair had been touched with licks of silver and she wore new spectacles with upswept frames. The new Jeremy found her unappealing, rather anemic.

Jeremy enjoyed himself. He moved back and forth between

Manufacture and Administration. Repeatedly he told people to carry on and not let him disturb them.

He was turning after having delivered this to his manager, when he once more found Miss Cox in his way.

She said, looking at his left shoulder, "I'm off for coffee now, Mr. Wood. It's eleven o'clock. Coffee break, you know."

"Of course."

Poor Miss Cox, Jeremy thought from the heights. No excitement in her life. Courting a clod. Future dreary, past a provincial ache, present a dullness that makes coffee breaks big deals.

"I shall take you," he stated, commanded.

Outside, he stepped to the van and opened its passenger door, saying, "We'll drive."

"But it's only a stone's throw, Mr. Wood."

"Ah, Miss Cox, but we are not going to the regular place."

"Really?"

"Enter my coach."

"Yes, Mr. Wood."

Happy in his grandness, Jeremy drove into town, located without surprise a parking metre impossibly alone, and, Miss Cox's elbow firmly in his hand, went into Bedford's largest hotel.

He was musing cynically over the single conversational exchange in the van, which had begun with his breezy, "How's the boyfriend, Miss Cox?"

"We've fallen out."

"Too bad."

The secretary said, "Estranged, you know."

"Yes."

"How's Mrs. Wood, Mr. Wood?"

"As a matter of fact." Pause.

"Yes?"

"As a matter of fact, we're estranged too."

"That's a shame," Miss Cox said tonelessly.

"Trial separation."

"What a good thing there are no kiddies."

"True."

Entering the hotel lobby, Jeremy dismissed the wonder of what had made him say that by telling himself he was an odd one, a character, a card, and an anarchist, plus a fellow of infinite jest and of endless surprises. As they entered the hotel's coffee shop, he gave a waiter a cool nod.

The lobby and coffee shop were as sumptuous as a Methodist's nightmare. Miss Cox and Jeremy sat, ordered, and partook of coffee and cakes. The secretary blinked at everything and looked suitably terrified.

Conversation was difficult. Not only were Jeremy and Miss Cox held at a considerable distance by the marble-topped table, but the reaching wings of their chairs acted as mufflers. Jeremy contented himself by wearing his amused expression.

Paying, he made sure Miss Cox saw his largesse. She seemed to borrow some of Jeremy's grandness when the waiter called her "madam." She was certainly beginning to look less impressed by the time they got up to leave.

Therefore, catching sight of a neon wriggle that informed COCKTAIL LOUNGE, Jeremy took his secretary by the arm and said, "Come along."

They went toward an archway. Miss Cox asked, "What, Mr. Wood? What?"

"A little drinky, my dear."

"Gosh."

"Help you drown your sorrows."

"I'm not. Norm's not that special. He's—" She broke off, lowered her voice, and hissed, "We can't go in there. Look."

Underneath the neon was a notice stating that this particular lounge was reserved for hotel residents only.

Jeremy, delighted, said, "Tish." His step and grip became firmer; and Miss Cox looked terrified again.

Apart from three waiters in red weskits and ruff shirts, the room was empty. Like a clown's laugh, it was rich and lifeless. The decor suggested that you pretend to be inside a Spanish castle. The tape playing George Shearing was as wrong as toes on a hand.

Jeremy and Miss Cox sat a corner table, a miniature refectory. They ordered sherries.

Jeremy leaned back and toyed with various judgematic phrases he had heard—"A mite harsh at the edges," "Friendly but somewhat immature." He decided not to bother. Instead, he began to talk loudly of the dream factory he would presently build.

Miss Cox had heard it all before, of course. Sitting upright on the rim of her seat, she shared her attention between Jeremy, her drink, and the room. Soon she relaxed and eased down on her look of awe.

Switching topics, Jeremy told of the time in the Underground train he had shouted that the world would end tomorrow.

Miss Cox said, "Gosh."

Jeremy bet himself that sometimes she said "golly."

She added, "What courage."

He lifted one shoulder. "Oh well."

"No, really, Mr. Wood. That takes courage and real strength of character. There aren't many people like you around. I must say I admire that sort of thing tremendously."

Jeremy crinkled his eyes like someone baby-sitting with a grandchild.

Miss Cox went on, "Think of all the people in the world who never do anything out of the ordinary. Such as me. Such as everyone I know. Well, you're not like that. You're one in a million, Mr. Wood."

Jeremy felt lovely. He basked in Miss Cox's blinking gaze as voluptuously as under a sunlamp. He was insouciant about draining his glass, and dribbled on his chin.

Wiping furtively with the back of his hand, he said, "There's a whole rich life waiting out there. One only needs to go out and get it."

"Yes, Mr. Wood. Yes. If one has the courage."

"True. It isn't easy. One will discover bad as well as good."

"Yes. Oh yes."

"Life is short, Miss Cox. Life is what we make it."

"That's very true," she said.

"We shouldn't let it rush by without enjoying it. Enjoying every minute of it."

"Some people just don't know how to live, do they?"

"What they need is to get out into the world. Out and seek. And what they might find, Miss Cox, is themselves."

"Oh yes. Yes yes."

"But they won't do it. Poor people."

"Poor them."

Jeremy shook his head sadly. He felt very wise. He also felt sorry again for the secretary. Watching her delicately empty her glass, he thought of how dull her existence was compared to his own.

He asked, "Another sherry?"

"Oh *no*, Mr. Wood," she said, giggling. "You are awful."

He chuckled. Immediately he realized he had never chuckled before. He decided at once that he would cultivate the habit. He would practise in private—it needed to be a little throatier.

"If I had another," Miss Cox said, "I'd be tiddly."

Stern, Jeremy said, "Nothing wrong with that."

"Thank you but no. Really."

The secretary looked so satisfyingly semifrightened again at the mere suggestion that Jeremy was willing to resist insisting. They left the lounge and went out to the street.

Playing a three-note sigh, Miss Cox said, "Ah well. Back to the grindstone."

"Fiddlesticks," Jeremy said. He gave an expansive smile. "We don't *have* to go back, my dear. I, after all, am the boss."

The secretary looked around nervously and then at her watch. "Oh, I don't know."

Jeremy smiled up at the sun. "It's such a beautiful day, I believe we'll go for a drive in the country."

"You're just . . . You're just . . ." Admiration had Miss Cox by the throat.

"Unusual," Jeremy suggested.

"Absolutely. I never met anyone like you before, Mr. Wood."

"Unconventional," Jeremy said. It was the word he had wanted in the first place.

"I'll say."

"Off we go, Miss Cox."

They returned to the van, and drove away and out of town. They were silent.

Out of town, he asked, "Where can we go to park and look at the view?"

Dumbly, Miss Cox pointed ahead. She kept on pointing for the next ten minutes. A final direction brought the van to a track through a copse. Where the trees ended there was a view of a narrow field and another copse. Jeremy stopped and switched off the engine.

The motor ticked like a bronchial clock, Miss Cox worked on clearing something from the back of her throat, and Jeremy stared at the skinny view.

So, he thought. Get on.

Sliding his arm along the back of the seat, he said, "Yes, very pretty."

"Thank you, Mr. Wood," the secretary said in a small, solemn voice. "The touch-up on the hair helps."

"Ah," Jeremy said. He told himself he had this fantastic knack of saying the right thing. It was a sort of genius. Some people just had it, that's all.

He moved closer. "You were pretty before, my dear." As he spoke the last two words he allowed his voice to stroll down to a roué huskiness.

Miss Cox cleared her throat again, though now with more squeak than rasp. Deliberately, she took off her spectacles and placed them on the dashboard.

Well, there you are, Jeremy thought.

He moved closer still, made body contact, and put his hand on the girl's farther shoulder. She turned to him. He kissed her on the mouth. Probing with his tongue, he met demure teeth. This he found highly erotic. He kissed around to her ear.

Jeremy's manliness and foresight were flattered when he realised that Miss Cox was trembling and panting.

"You shouldn't," she gasped.

Jeremy looked with one eye at the van's roomy body and its flooring of felt. He said, "Let's get in the back."

"We shouldn't, Mr. Wood."

"Just for a minute."

"Well . . ."

He moved back and gave her his hand. She followed into the back. Miss Cox, huddled on the floor with legs tucked underneath, was having trouble with her throat again. Jeremy put both arms around her and drew her down supine, she all the while giving a whine of protest.

Jeremy semicovered her upper body with his. He kissed her. Miss Cox was as lax as a sleeper in training, apart from her tremor. Jeremy felt wonderfully like a rapist with a petrified schoolgirl. This was heightened every time the secretary gasped, between kisses, "No. Please. No."

During the next step in the procedure, the Jeremy of old, last week's Jeremy, would have been true to his Anglo-Saxon ethos. He would have worked by touch, would have gone to elaborate lengths to avoid the embarrassment and freakishness of using his eyes. Not the new Jeremy.

He pushed up to his knees. He smiled down at Miss Cox, who turned her head to the side and glared at the bodywork and whispered, "No."

Jeremy said, "Yes."

"No no."

Jeremy paused to enjoy the view.

Jeremy returned to his task.

He knelt upright. Miss Cox gasped, whimpered at the roof, and said "no" to the other side of the van.

Jeremy steered by touch, found the way, and set to work.

Miss Cox was as still as a tree in a light breeze; there was only that surface flutter. Her head turned away, she said, "Stop."

Jeremy had no mind for the lack of response, nor for the want of embrace. It was a mental act.

He was nearing the end of the ride. Suddenly, Miss Cox clamped her arms around his neck, slammed her face next to his, and yelled:

"Do me, Mr. Wood! Do me do me!"

Jeremy spent, surgingly, like a drunken sailor. As with a sneeze, first cousin of the present spasm, he was briefly lost to the world. He returned to hear Miss Cox gurgling.

Five awkward minutes later, Jeremy and his secretary were back in the front seat. Another fifteen, and they were drawing up outside the factory. Although there had been no words exchanged, they had taken turns at throat clearing.

They went into Administration. Miss Cox to her desk, Jeremy to take leave of his manager. He was recovering from his loss of personality during the aftermath. He became hearty. He shook the manager's hand as if it were a pan of scrambled eggs and when at the door threw Miss Cox a roguish glance.

Christ, he thought, driving off. Bloody hell. By God. What a devil the man is. What a card.

Over the following hour, until it palled, he relived the sexual bout. Then he hummed, tapped a tight-shod foot, and enjoyed the drive. He looked at the trees from time to time and thought how attractive they were.

※※※※※

Alice was nervous as she went into the bathroom. Noon had just struck, which meant that now she should get ready to go to her rendezvous.

This, she thought, will never do. She would have to close her mind to the excitement and danger that lay ahead.

The decision worked well. In the shower she thought only of lathering and rinsing. During the final rinse, long and luxurious, she began to sing.

In common with a hundred and forty-eight million other people, Alice secretly believed she had a unique voice, a voice of unsurpassable tonal purity. She was convinced that had she been taken on early enough by a teacher of renown (in Vienna, of course) in order to learn technicalities, she would by this time be appearing in the great opera houses of the world. Alice experienced regret for fifteen seconds every day.

That over now, she had Madam Butterfly in a killing bottle. She swooped and trilled and quavered. Calling herself Mimi, she hit a high note. It skittered abruptly into a scream, as if terrified.

Alice chopped it off. Embarrassed, she stuck her capped head under the jets. She pretended that not only was she someone else but also that she hadn't heard a thing.

Switching off the taps, Vienna forgotten until tomorrow, Alice stepped from the shower and embraced a towel. Next came talcum. She felt as warm and comforted as the puppy in the middle.

While brushing out her hair, Alice let loose of her decision. The excitement came back. She stared at herself in the mirror—aghast. What she was about to do was incredibly underhanded.

She found that she was brushing her ear. Closed mind, she told herself.

Alice went into the bedroom to set about dressing. She chose a peasant skirt, which would serve well the farmer smock, which worked nicely under the grandee jacket, which could be topped off with a queenly scarf.

Had Alice realised the ensemble's significance, she would have reversed it, then fretted over the result—hearing tumbril wheels —and tried to play out from the middle. Fortunately for her peace of mind, she always dressed by colour, and stayed away from black and white.

Ready, Alice unprimmed the curtains. Her glance fell on the backing house. She sighed and shook her head. Like the irrepressibly jovial, Mr. Barlow was a worry.

Only the other evening, Alice thought, he had looked so ill, sprawled out on a deck chair with his hand to his brow and his feet tapping together as if to fight the pain. Finally she had stepped over the wall and sat on it so that she could question him firmly about his arthritis. Although he had protested his fitness, you could see the suffering. It was clear in his groaning and in the way his head drooped sideways until it almost touched the ground.

He might be all right, though, with those new pills. And could be he was simply a bad patient. Men generally were. Men were such funny creatures altogether. There was no understanding them. Even the steady Jeremy had been acting odd lately. Henry was a funny one too.

The night before, Henry Mastin had come for his bridge lesson. He was an apt pupil—so apt that he won a trial game. The next minute, however, he was asking if the clubs were those red discs with pointed bottoms and dented tops.

Going on all the time was his roundabout manner of showing gratitude for the lessons, using flattery and confidences. He kept saying how pretty she was, and what a nice figure, and such slim ankles; several times he patted her knee, just like a little boy; once he blurted in a muffled way that at home he was starved for six, but before she could ask six what he had gone back to talking about those red discs; the pendant in the neckline of her blouse he examined closely and at length, saying admiring things yet referring to it in the plural, as if it were a pair; at the door, leaving, he massaged her back for a moment (he must have guessed how it ached when she played for long) and then fled in shyness when she kissed him on the cheek. A funny one, Henry.

Alice was still standing at the window. She congratulated herself on how well she was doing with the closed mind, thinking of Mr. Barlow and Henry Mastin instead of the rendezvous. But she couldn't hold it any longer. The time had come to go.

Alice twitched. She stopped stifling her emotions. The nervousness and excitement rushed in like anti-angel fools. She also felt guilty.

Leaving the room, she went downstairs and outside. She began to walk. From the pocket of her skirt she brought a piece of paper to check the address—in case she had misread it on the other seventy-seven checks. It was still 10 Carpet Street.

Alice shivered. She had never done anything like this before. Was she going to go through with it, go all the way? Well, yes. Would she do it again another time? Well, it depended if she enjoyed it or not.

What if Jeremy should find out!

Alice had a good mind to turn around and go right back. The fact that she'd promised faithfully to be there kept her walking. She just hoped it wouldn't show on her face later when she went to Miss Tomkin's.

Alice crossed the High Street, climbed an alley, and along a street replete with side turnings. One of these was called Carpet. She entered.

There were betrayed-looking villas on either side. Tall Victorians, only one or two were in brave repair, as if refusing to accept that the empire had gone.

Number ten hadn't made up its mind: though some of the window frames were painted and the doormat was new, a card that offered a room to let added that the desired tenants should be gentlefolk.

Nervous, Alice pulled the bell handle. The clang inside started brisk footsteps. They stopped. The door was opened by an attractive girl in her twenties. She appeared to be in the grip of pleasure at being able to be sternly officious.

She asked a cruel, "Yes?"

Alice said, "Hello. I'm supposed to meet Mavis Jones here."

"The name?"

"Mrs. Alice Wood."

The girl's pleasure increased. "Mizzz," she said.

"Sorry. Mizzz."

"Yes, I have your name. Welcome, sister, to this meeting of the Secret Provisionals of the Women's Liberation Movement, Local Seventeen."

"How kind of you to say so."

The girl refused to unstern. "Now all I need is the password. This week's."

Alice looked doubtful. Her guilt increased. "Do I actually have to say it?"

"'Fraid so."

Alice swallowed. As far under her breath as she could go, she muttered, "Down with husbands."

"Come in."

Along a passage they went and through a door. They were met by a blast of shrill voices. The owners came into view as Alice followed down basement steps. Below was a tightly packed throng of female heads. It was like a large and hairy animal, this yak of women.

Alice, only vaguely aware of externals, was fervently thinking: Forgive me, Jeremy. Please forgive me.

On Saturday afternoon, Jeremy walked through Hampstead. He was slowly turning from a husband of guilty starts and cheat-winning smiles, into a man of the world.

By the time he was three quarters of the way from home, the conversion was complete. Unknown to Jeremy, it had been helped by Friday's exchange, which his subconscious had taken and planted with fingers of a perennial green.

"Henry was sharp last night," Alice had said. "It's amazing how quickly he's picking up the game."

"Smart man, old Mastin."

"Well no, not especially. At any rate, not as smart as you."

"You're a good teacher then. Yes, of course you are."

"It's not that, darling. It's simply that bridge is easy to learn if only one concentrates."

"Ah."

"I could teach you in no time at all."

"What's for dinner?" Jeremy had asked, meaning: No, thank you. No cards, no Red Ass.

All that, however, was forgotten. He was also, as usual, forgetting his guilt. He even mused once, lightly, that he was a three-timing louse.

Nevertheless, Jeremy had firmed his decision to spend only ten minutes with Mona Mastin. A small, heel-sized part of his soul had pleaded; the larger part had been adamant. There was to be no more of that nonsense.

The same went for Miss Cox. An unplanned roll in the hay was one thing, Jeremy had thought, a connivance at continuing sex quite another. And that was all he had thought about it. There had been none of the endless moralising that had followed his first shafting of fidelity. Much of his spare time had been spent in the practise of chuckling.

He came to the house. It stood there grotesquing in sunlight, as unlikely as a weed with frail roots. Walking the path, he went inside. Compared to the week before, Jeremy was a mammoth of cool; compared to normalcy, he was nervous.

Climbing the stairs, he reminded himself of the excuses he had thought up for getting away quickly:

A stew he had left on the stove (his wife out). An uncle coming for tea. A neighbour's child, crippled, whom he had promised to take to the pictures. A blind old lady he should read to. And diarrhea.

Another one he rather fancied was pretending he had a premonition that his house was on fire. It could be done with flair, drama. It had a marvellous touch of the mystical. He could gaze into space suddenly and raise a pincered hand to his brow and say odd things—before rushing out. But the problem was, he would look silly afterwards, later, on account of no fire.

Jeremy reached the flat door. As he knocked, he told himself he could always claim to have arrived home in the nick of time and done valiant battle with a fire extinguisher. He could wear a bandage on his hand, romantic. He could limp a bit. He could . . .

The door swung in. Revealed was Mona Mastin, sagging kindly. Her hair was down, and she wore a red robe and pink slippers. Never before had she been so fetching.

She smiled as if at a deed to heaven. In a soft, organ drawl she said, "Well, hello there."

Jeremy would have curled his toes under had there been room. He said, "Good afternoon."

"A divine afternoon."

"Sorry I'm late."

"Only a few minutes. A delicious agony of waiting."

"Yes."

"Do come in, Jeremy."

She turned and he followed. He was aware of perfume from Mona and canine snuffles from the kitchen.

In the living room the curtains were drawn, the lamps gave a low cozy light, and the electric fire was burning red. Jeremy realised that his resolve, his will, would be tested to the full.

He stood by the end of the couch. Mona joined him and handed him a drink. It was brandy. He wondered who would be the first to speak and what would the matter be. But he was not uncomfortable, not this new Jeremy. He was not searching for verbal gambits like a TV addict in a black-out.

He said calmly, "Nice weather."

"To be indoors," Mona said, her eyes wicked over the glass.

"Quite. Yes. Just so."

"And with someone special."

Jeremy nodded. In there, his head, a clock seemed to be ticking. He felt strong, resolute.

Jeremy finished his drink. Mona took the glass, put it aside with her own, and went to the front of the couch. She said, "Come where it's warm."

Jeremy moved forward, asking, "Did you see that documentary on telly last night?"

Mona said, "I do like a man with a sense of humour."

"Yes," he muttered. "Well."

Mona gave him a lingering smile. Then she turned away; body first, face last. She slipped the robe off her shoulders, down to her waist, and around to the front.

Jeremy told himself he couldn't very well do a sudden gaze into space if she wasn't watching.

Mona bent forward gracefully. She folded the robe onto a stool, doing the job with slow care as if the material held a sleeping infant. The clock in his head slowed its tick to a crawl.

Mona straightened. Languidly she turned. She raised her arms and moved forward.

Jeremy snapped his eyes away. But before he could fix them into anything like a gaze, Mona was upon him. She embraced him hard and began kissing him with ardour.

He clenched his fists firmly at his sides. He was terribly resolute. Now, he thought, was the moment. The cerebral clock picked up speed.

Jeremy tongued Mona's tongue out of his mouth and said, "Uncle." Her lips came swarmingly back. He twisted free and gasped, "Old and crippled. Stew." His mouth was captured again. He felt a familiar tension, and was furious. The clock above was chattering like teeth in a basin.

Jeremy wrenched his head backwards. Pain stabbed his neck. He said, "Ouch!"

"What, love?"

"Fire."

"Mmm?"

"House on."

Mona closed in again and claimed his mouth. He unclenched his fists and stopped the clock. To hell with it, he thought. One more time wouldn't hurt.

Jeremy circled her hips and spread his hands—

There was a thud in the hallway.

There's a thud in the hallway, a mental voice said to Jeremy. Of Mona he asked, "Did you hear that thud in the hallway?"

"No."

"Well, there was a thud in the hallway."

Now came another. Louder.

"Yes," Mona said, moving back to a loose embrace. "It's the people in the next flat." She sounded as if she didn't believe it.

She and Jeremy turned to stare at the door. Jeremy's eyes were fixed. He had a horrible feeling. It was like a premonition.

The door opened.

Into the room came Henry Mastin.

ᴗᴗᴗᴗᴗ

After Mona's arms had flopped free of Jeremy, there was no movement for some seconds from any of the three people. The period seemed endless, like a child's week.

The three were open-mouthed and disbelieving.

Jeremy stared at Henry Mastin, who had stopped on the threshold. Mastin gaped at his naked wife. Mona showed a half smile of ridicule at this impossibility as she stared at her husband.

Now, belief approached. Movement creaked into being.

Henry Mastin flicked his eyes between the visitor and Mona, from face to face, from nude body to dressed body. His arms twitched. A deep royal-red flush rose from inside his collar.

Mona's smile began to switch on and off. She folded her arms as if collecting up a small Arab tent, and, in one continuous movement, ran the crossed hands aloft her cheeks, resting there.

Jeremy was terrified. He was aghast. Also, as part of his fear, he was fascinated by the colour in which Henry Mastin was drowning.

Mona patted and squeezed her cheeks, and forced her lips into an out-thrust to match her eyes. She emitted a noise like that of an impolite stallion.

Jeremy's throat tightened. He felt as though he were being garotted. He could not have uttered a word to gain a pension. His first movement in this dying tableau was unconscious, though it stemmed from awareness of the nudity beside him.

He lowered both hands, spread flat, and covered his groin.

Henry Mastin was now full to the hairline brim. At once the colour started to drain. It did so swiftly but left dregs in and around his eyes. The white face was lifeless.

Still windy, Mona gave a horrid belchlike moan.

Jeremy swallowed rapidly and fought off the invisible garotter. Speech, he yammered to himself, was vital.

Wobbling, Mona settled to a kneel. Next she sat back on her heels; sat small. Both hands were still firmly warding off sight and smell.

Jeremy spoke. He said in a thin pale voice, "There's been a terrible mistake."

Henry Mastin seemed not to hear.

"I can explain everything," Jeremy piped. "It's the stew."

Mastin's gaze came to rest on a nearby table. Piled there were half-a-dozen books. Mastin stepped across, lifted a volume, glanced as if out of habit at its spine, then looked up and took aim at his wife.

Jeremy said gaspingly, "Fire." And, "No no."

Mastin threw the book at Mona. It missed. Listlessly, he picked up the other books one at a time and threw them at his wife. They all missed.

Jeremy began to back away.

Henry Mastin found a pencil. He threw it, dart fashion. It bounced off Mona's head. She squeaked.

"Blind uncle," Jeremy babbled thinly. "Stew." He stopped retreating as he felt his back touch the curtains. He stood there shrunken and pigeon-toed, body bent forward from the hips, hands over his crotch.

Jeremy had never been so frightened in his life. The fear was a terrible silence inside him. At its zenith, it was like the sound of one knee knocking.

He said a placating, "Diarrhea."

Henry Mastin had moved to another table. It held a folded scarf. He picked this up and threw it. While his aim was fair, he was betrayed by his missile. The scarf opened up midway and floated down like a wounded parachute.

Mastin lifted the table itself, a frail creature on long legs. He tossed it, now using more vigour. The table clattered against Mona's thighs. She squeaked, swayed, moaned.

Jeremy feebled, "Now now."

With muted eagerness Mastin stepped to a picture on the wall and took hold of the frame. It refused to come free. He moved on, reached the hearth, and scanned the mantel's collection of small objects. He was now some three feet from where Mona sat.

"Easy does it," Jeremy mumbled. He was wondering if it would help if he closed his eyes.

An expression of subjugated triumph limped across Mastin's face: he had seen the stool that held Mona's robe. It was stubby, heavy, formed of natural oak.

Jeremy's fear divided so that half could be for Mona. He knew he should act to draw Mastin's attention away, even to himself. He stayed still, but whispered, "Come come."

Henry Mastin bent down, shoved the robe off the stool, took a leg in each hand, and rose. His arms went on rising until the stool was on high.

"Really now," Jeremy said.

Henry Mastin moved forward. He stood beside his wife. He brought the stool down heavily. It thunked in the centre of Mona's head.

Jeremy gasped, "Aaggh!"

The impact sent Mona's hands flying from their place like shot birds. Her head dropped, her arms dropped, and she fell over sideways.

The meagre display of life left Henry Mastin's face. He let the stool drop to the floor, where it lay with its legs up. Distantly, Jeremy was offended.

Mastin moved to the couch. He stepped up onto the seat as though it were a high kerb. Turning on bouncy feet, he sank to a squat against the back, knees to chest. He put his thumb in his mouth and fixed blank eyes on the hearth.

"Well," Jeremy ventured. He straightened. The storm, he felt, was over, the danger gone. His fear ran off like water from wool, leaving only a surface glisten.

He said, "Now see what you've done."

Mastin ignored him.

Jeremy went forward. He dropped to one knee beside the motionless Mona, and shook her and patted her cheek and murmured encouragement. There was no response.

Reaching for the robe, he covered the huddled, naked body. He continued with his ministrations.

Two minutes later, after using every test he knew, Jeremy reached the top of his growing surprise: Mona Mastin was dead. He pulled up the robe to cover her face.

Calm drenched him like a shower. He was sodden with a chill tranquility. Standing, he looked at Henry Mastin, who was still enjoying his thumb, and said:

"You've killed your wife, old man. Sorry."

Mastin turned his head slowly. Jeremy repeated his statement. Henry Mastin took his thumb out, wiped it absently on his sleeve, and said, "Oh?"

"She's *dead*, old man. Really dead."

"I see."

Jeremy wagged a finger. "Get that into your head."
"Okay."
"She's dead and you've got to do something about it."
"Yes."
Jeremy semisnapped, "For God's sake, man, wake up."
Henry Mastin blinked, twitched. "I am. I am."
"You've killed your wife."
"I know. Awkward."
"Do you want to call the police?" Jeremy asked, and immediately added, "No, of course not. It was an accident. In a way. You didn't mean to do it. It's not really—well—murder."
"No."
"Not that at all."
Mastin said tonelessly, "I didn't mean to do it."
"Certainly not."
"It was an accident, you see."
"Right. So no police."
"No."
Relieved, Jeremy set to work. Vaguely astounded at his calmness and efficiency, he took the empty glasses into the kitchen, where, watched balefully by Rover, he washed them and put them away.

In the hallway he stopped and closed his eyes to reconstruct earlier movement. He decided he could not have left his fingerprints anywhere else. Also, he swiftly cancelled out footprints, shreds of cloth, and hats with his name inside. He returned to the living room and with his handkerchief wiped the stool legs.

Henry Mastin asked politely, "She's dead, eh?"
"Yes."
"Passed on?"
"Absolutely."
Pushing himself up, Mastin sat atop the couch back. "What're we going to do?"
"You have to do something, you certainly do. And I think I have a solution for you."
"Good show."
"I'm going to help you," Jeremy said, and left the sentence hanging there, holding back the fire of, "Because I don't want it known that I was involved."

"You'll help me?"
"I will."
"Thanks."
"You're welcome."
"Decent of you."
"What you'll do is this," Jeremy said. "You'll make it look like a robbery."
"We have been burgled twice, matter of fact."
"Good."
"And I'm going to be sick in a minute."
"Hold on."
"All right."

Jeremy went out and found the bedroom. Careful of prints, he pulled out drawers and scattered their contents. He untidied the wardrobe. He flung the mattress off the bed. Using his knuckles, he upended a handbag, found some loose banknotes, took them back to the living room with him, and stuffed them into Mastin's top pocket.

After drawing the curtains and switching off the lamps and electric fire, he went to Mona and lifted the robe. "Help me put this on her."

"All right," Mastin said. He made no move.

Jeremy got on with the job himself, rolling and lugging the floppy weight. He thought it somehow treacherous of Rover not to howl.

He said, "Tell them she often wore just this around the house."
"Yes."
"But it's unimportant. What they'll think is, she caught the burglar in the act and he killed her."
"I daresay."

Still thinking about Rover so that he wouldn't think of Mona, Jeremy asked, "What made you come home anyway?"
"Didn't believe you."
"What?"
"I didn't believe you'd be here. Wanted to prove it."
"This, by the way, it was all in innocent fun."
"Oh yes?" Mastin said. He sounded as he looked, disinterested.
"I dared her to take the robe off, for a joke. She did it."
"I see."

Jeremy asked, "Did you go to the football match?"
"No."
"Then you didn't buy a ticket."
"Got one for the season."
"Good."
"Oh?"

Jeremy got the robe on. Not once during the operation had he looked at Mona's face. Leaving the body in a sprawl, he stood up, glanced around, and nodded.

"Right," he said. "Let's go."
"Go?"

Jeremy took Mastin's arm, pulled him to his feet and off the couch, and led him out to the hall. At the flat door he asked, "Did anyone see you come in? Neighbours, someone you know?"

"Don't think so."

"Right. Now look. We'll leave quietly and unobtrusively. When we're away from here we'll separate. You go to somewhere near the football ground. When the crowd leaves, come home, find your wife, phone the police. There's no need to mention me at all. Understand?"

"Yes."
"Sure?"
"Yes."

Jeremy tilted his head at the lock. "How the burglar got in, we'll let the police puzzle that one out."

Henry Mastin said, "Skeleton."

Jeremy patted his arm, relieved that he was beginning to think. "Sorry about Mona, old man."

"Thank you very much."

Jeremy knuckled back the catch and opened the door. Outside was clear. They slipped out and went downstairs, meeting no one.

At the end of the street they separated without a word or glance. Jeremy stopped by a tree to look back. He watched Henry Mastin until he was out of sight.

Suddenly Jeremy found himself hugging the tree with both arms. He was trembling uncontrollably.

FIVE

Alice left the supermarket, around which she had travelled at a sensible three and a half miles an hour. Being midweek, Wednesday, the aisles had been quiet and safe. Only once had danger threatened—a flighty young girl with her head in the clouds—and that Alice had avoided with some adroit swerving.

In jeans, checked shirt, and head scarf, Alice looked flightily young herself. She bounced along swinging the string bag that held her supermarket purchase, a can of beans. Her face, however, bore the marks of strain. The past few days had been difficult.

Like all those whose emotions were fed sparingly by externals —the lonely, the old, actors—Alice had seized, with unseemly eagerness on the advent of true drama, a tragedy that came close to home.

Crossing the road at traffic lights, the while refusing to look at a woman driver, Alice went on. She saw over the way a familiar face, one from Horsetrough Lane. Giving a wave, she thought with pleasure of Saturday evening.

They had picketed the Town Hall again. This time the results were more positive. Inside the building were two cleaning women and a man in a boiler suit. They watched from a window for at least fifteen minutes. Before withdrawing, one of the women shook a fist.

A photographer from the Hampstead *Monthly Crier* had come. He was sympathetic to the cause. Alice ordered half a dozen of the six-by-fours.

Slow but sure progress, she thought now, smiling. Her smile

had the wan quality she had unconsciously cultivated over the past days.

Her face became solemn as she remembered—again, for the twentieth time—that while the picketing was going on, right then, at that very moment, the police were investigating. Which, she mused acutely, just went to show.

She reduced her bounce and the swing of her bag. Had she been able to bring it off, she would have changed the colour of her clothing to grey.

Alice spotted another familiar face, this on a man with whom she occasionally played cards. He was coming out of a shop ahead, snarling at the lettuce he was trying to get into a basket.

Alice changed course, aiming for the shop. She imagined she was not thinking: This time it's bound to happen. It should have happened before by rights. It can't go on and on not happening.

Jaw jutted, the man beat his lettuce. He was tall and middle-aged and had a prominent hairline. Neatly, conservatively dressed, he nevertheless bore that haunted look of the bridge addict and the bomb-disposal expert.

Alice stopped and said, "Mr. Reed. Good afternoon."

"Hello, my dear."

"Nice day."

"Yes," he said, adding, "And you're looking in the pink of good health."

Which of course was silly, mere flattering nonsense, for Alice knew perfectly well that she was peaked. No one could miss seeing that.

The man said, "I'm looking pretty fit myself."

Alice shook her head, admitting, "I am managing to bear up."

The thing was, you had to be asked. Telling people point-blank wasn't right. There were masses of friends she could have telephoned or visited, and told, and she had telephoned and had visited, but not one of them had asked. Some people were funny that way.

So it had not happened yet. And Alice had the dead feeling that once more it was not going to happen: Enquirer: "Whatever is the matter, Mrs. Wood, you look so awful." Alice: "Something dreadful occurred to a friend of mine the other day." "Really?" "Yes." "What?" "She was murdered."

"Yes, I'm pretty fit," Mr. Reed said. "Considering."
"Yes, I am too, considering. Considering Saturday."
"Last night. You won't believe what my partner played."
"Saturday afternoon, to be exact."
"After that game, I didn't sleep a wink."
Alice made her eyes tortured. "Don't talk about sleep."

Mr. Reed didn't. Clasping Alice's sleeve and leaning close, he named in a low voice all the cards he had held in the disastrous partnership. Only another addict would have bothered to listen, and only a fanatic would have registered the details.

Alice, by nature good, sighed into submission. She put on a fair show of attentiveness, nodding, while consoling herself with the fact that later today Mr. Barlow would be back from his long weekend of water-taking at a spa. He wouldn't let her down, especially if she managed a bit of coughing as well.

Alice recalled another consoler. She had been the first to know, before Jeremy. *And* that was after he had missed the item altogether. So there.

Sunday morning, they had been sprawled around the living room with the newspapers. After a while, they exchanged. Alice saw the small item footing the front page. Stiffening, feeling a growing heat, she read its few lines over and over.

She stood with care, made her posture neat, and said in a calm voice, "Jeremy darling. Prepare yourself for a shock."

"Huh?"

"A shock."

He looked up from his sit on the floor. "What is it?"

"Take a grip on yourself, darling."

"I have done."

"It's your best friend's wife. Henry's wife."

"Henry Mastin?"

"The same."

"Well, go on."

Alice shuddered. "Darling, she's been murdered."

"My God," Jeremy said, staring up. "My God." He raised a hand and pressed its back against his brow. "My God." His other hand he brought up to clasp his throat. "My God."

"It's terrible, I know."

"Old Mastin's wife murdered."

"Yes."
"On Friday."
"No, Saturday."
"Murdered out on the street."
Alice corrected, "In her flat, actually."
"Poor Mastin's wife. Shot to death."
"Blunt instrument, it says."
"My God," Jeremy rasped. "Beaten to death in the early hours of the morning."
"Afternoon, they think."
"Killed while working away in her own kitchen."
"It doesn't say."
"Probably working away in her kitchen, fully dressed and everything."
"I don't know."
"And poor old Mastin there, trying to fight off the attacker."
"No, he was out. He found the body when he came home."
"My God."

Jeremy was so deeply affected that he needed to go upstairs and lie down with the room darkened. Alice was loving and solicitous. She agreed with him every time he said he couldn't believe it. That was all he did say, and weakly, except for when she asked how long he had known the victim.

"No no no," he said. "No."

"Mmm?"

"I never met her."

At that Alice experienced a curious feeling, almost like disappointment, which she knew must be indigestion (those heavy Sunday breakfasts). She said, "Oh."

The same feeling was upon her now. If she forgot it, she thought, it would probably go away. Alice looked at Mr. Reed's busily talking mouth and tried to concentrate. She was lost in a maze of symbols and numbers.

Therefore, furtively in respect of her most conscious self, Alice imagined that Mr. Reed was asking why she looked so pale and so peaked and imagined telling him it was because a close friend had been brutally slain.

"But how terrible, my dear."

"It hasn't been easy."

"I can see that. What torment."

"Yes."

"It must have been the murder here in Hampstead. I read about it."

"Yes, it's been in the papers every day. Bits. But we have the inside story. My husband has telephoned Henry frequently. That's the husband of the slain."

"You send shudders down my spine."

"The inquest was this morning. They brought in a verdict of murder by person or persons unknown. We should have gone, I suppose, and we should go to the funeral tomorrow, but my husband says it's not the thing to do, Henry must work this out on his own two feet."

"Person or persons unknown," Mr. Reed said musingly.

"Yes, but the police know the type. A burglar. He got in through a window, was caught in the act by dear Mona—Mrs. Mastin—who'd just got up from a nap, and he killed her. The murder weapon, they believe, was an iron bar. And he wore gloves."

"Ah. Yes. Mmm."

"There was no sexual assault, despite her state of undress. That's how the police know he was a professional burglar—another clue to that was his way with dogs. He was only after money and valuables. But there was nothing in the place worth taking, apart from a handful of pounds. He killed for almost nothing. Obviously he's got a long police record, and if caught robbing would go to prison for many years."

"The poor woman. Poor husband."

"Yes. And just think, Henry was at my house only two evenings before. Sitting there as happy as could be. Little did he know then that his wife would soon be taken from his life by violence. Little did any of us know. Jeremy was terribly cut up. He's been as quiet as quiet since then. Stoic, you know. I have too. Very stoic."

"All you have said has shocked and impressed me. Deeply."

That was just about it. Alice no longer had indigestion. Cheerfully she plugged in to Mr. Reed saying, his face poppingly incredulous: "*Hearts.* He played a *heart.* I nearly screamed."

"It's shattering, I know."
"I didn't sleep a wink."

Alice patted his shoulder, looked at her watch, and backed away. "Must be off, Mr. Reed. I'm going to meet Jeremy at the Underground station."

"And then in the next game . . ."

"'Bye," said firmly.

※※※※※

Like drunken rabbits chasing through a warren, the train swayed along its tunnel. Each lurch increased the passengers' look of outraged satisfaction. They tightened mouths and nostrils, and seemed to be hoping for a lurch beyond the point of no return.

Only Jeremy Wood was without grimness. This despite the fact that he was strap-hanging, an act he hated because his height necessitated a reach so high that it pulled up his jacket and exposed the seat of his pants. There was nothing so silly-looking, he always thought, as the seat of a man's pants.

Jeremy was wearing his nonbusiness clothes, as he had been all week. He simply lacked the interest in his work to change for it. He was too preoccupied.

Jeremy had borne up well under the strain. After that attack of nerves in the street outside the Mastin flat, he had returned to being the new Jeremy. The sole problem had been Alice.

But at the moment he was thinking of Miss Cox.

Monday, Jeremy had found waiting for him at work a letter from the Bedford secretary. In flowery language, every other word a petal, the matter stated that Miss Cox's world was rosy and good, that on a recent occasion in a certain vehicle she had reached a height of emotion never before visited, and that she was counting the hours until Friday. The letter also said that you were only young once.

Jeremy had been smug, blasé; and lordly with Mrs. Hendon. The letter he had flushed down the lavatory at day's end, after a final read of that bit about emotional heights.

Until the train clacked into Hampstead, he thought of Miss Cox, once sourly, recalling his decision to end the inchoate affair. It was the trembling and panting he would miss most.

Jeremy alighted and went up to street level. On seeing Alice waiting, he first perked with pleasure, next sighed in resignation.

"Darling."

"Darling."

"How nice of you to meet me."

Alice crinkled her eyes and linked his arm. "Did you call Henry today?"

Here we go. Can't leave it alone for a minute.

He said, "Yes. Nothing new. You've been shopping, I see."

"I do think, dear, that we should go and call on him. It's the proper thing to do."

Oh sure. Lovely. Go there and have the police, who were sure to be hanging about, start asking questions as to one's relationship with the deceased, or have a neighbour say I know that man, it all comes back to me now, he was here on Saturday.

Jeremy said, "No, darling." He went on to repeat his arguments for leaving Henry Mastin alone, none of which made sense.

"True," Alice said disagreeably. "Anyway, at least we should have sent a letter of condolence."

"I already did. Days ago."

"Oh." Alice had the expression of someone arriving for a party the night after.

He was lying, just as he had been lying about having telephoned Mastin earlier. He had called Mastin once only since the fateful afternoon, to find out if all was running smoothly. In return he had received one telephone call from the other man, who had rambled in cryptic fashion like a hiker who goes backwards. Jeremy was more determined than ever to avoid his ex-partner in intrigue. Besides, he had the weird feeling that Henry Mastin might say, "A bargain's a bargain. I killed my wife, now you've got to kill yours."

Alice said, "Really, we should do something. Really. If we can't go there, we should have him over."

"All in good time, darling."

"Tomorrow evening, perhaps. When you're away. The usual Thursday thing. Except instead of cards I could give him a square meal."

"Mm."

"The poor man's probably not eating properly. A good feed and a sympathetic ear, that's what he needs."

It sounded safe enough, Jeremy thought. He said, "All right."

Alice jiggled his arm. "Good."

"How was your day, dear?"

"Fine. Did Henry say there'd been anything new in the case?"

"No. I see you got my favourite beans."

It went on like that all the way to Horsetrough Lane. Alice even came up with a new one. Could it be possible that she and Jeremy had met the Mastins sometime, and forgotten?—yes, of course it was. They must have met.

On reaching home, Jeremy escaped at once with Fifi to the Heath. He breathed free. Smiling, he thought about emotional heights and the counting of hours.

At one point in his walk, passing a copse, Jeremy thought he caught through the trees a glimpse of Henry Mastin. Just the thought was enough. Jeremy hurried off in the other direction, taking short and rapid steps to hide the fact that he was running. Strollers stared. Jeremy felt a fool.

Back home, he gobbled dinner. Afterwards, he pretended vast, deaf-to-everything-else interest in a television programme.

He went early to bed.

It was the next morning, in the shop, that the new Jeremy sauntered cruelly away. This permitted entry of the long-term reaction to the killing of Mona Mastin. Jeremy fell into a mental mistiness. He felt flat, disspirited.

For the first time, he began to live again the death scene. He was aghast. The more often he saw it—the stool, the blow, the fallen body—the more dazed and disbelieving he became. It seemed incredible that he, Jeremy Wood of Horsetrough Lane and Wood's Rustic Furniture, had been a witness to a murder. A murder!

Once he went into the lavatory to stare at himself in the mirror. He simply did not look the part. The whole thing was fantastic.

The only point Jeremy declined to dwell on, or even approach, was that he had been a party to the crime—indeed, the catalyst.

His employees he avoided or warned off with heavy frowns, as if they were friends fresh back from exotic vacations. At lunchtime he stayed away for two hours, sitting in gloom over long-lasting beers.

Jeremy decided as the day grew to middle-age that he would not go to Bedford. He told himself this was due both to fidelity and to concern for Miss Cox's feelings. He told himself he was certainly not influenced by the recurring vision of the ex-boyfriend bursting into the van and beating Miss Cox to death.

He went to a hotel, feeling noble and virtuous and a martyr.

On Friday Alice reported, to Jeremy's vague registration, that Henry Mastin had turned up as arranged, looking really awful. He had been taciturn and without appetite. When he did talk, it had been oddly. But after all, the poor soul had just buried his wife.

Jeremy was still in shock. With brief visits from the new man, it continued for some time. He was listless. When Mrs. Hendon informed him that a Mr. Mastin had telephoned three times during the lunch hour, Jeremy shrugged and said, "Who cares?"

On Sunday morning the Woods, in pajamas and robes, were at their customary sloth of reading the newspapers. The telephone rang as Alice was saying for the tenth time, "It's not mentioned anywhere. Not a word." Jeremy got up to answer.

He identified his number. A female voice said, "Is that Mr. J. Wood?"

"Speaking."

"Oh good. I'm so relieved."

"Who is this, please?"

The voice said, "I'm Miss Cox."

Jeremy ducked his head, as if quickly swallowing a bitter pill. He said, "Well now."

"I'm here."

"What?"

"I'm here, Mr. Wood. Here in London."

"Ah," Jeremy said. He glared at the wall.

"I came down yesterday. I'm staying at the Palace in Bayswater Road. It's taken me this long to get up the nerve to call you."

New Jeremy to the rescue. He covered the mouthpiece and said, loudly, "I understand, Mr. Green." Hand off, he said, "Ah."

"I was worried when you didn't show up on Thursday night. Well, you know, when you weren't there Friday. Are you all right?"

"Perfectly."

"Oh, I'm so relieved, Mr. Wood. I'd been thinking all kinds. Accidents and everything."

Hand on: "I see, Mr. Green."

Miss Cox asked, "But why didn't you come?"

Hand off: "Business."

"Of course."

"That's right, Mr. Green."

"Who?"

Jeremy got a twinge of pain between the eyes. "Nothing."

Miss Cox said, "Well, look, Mr. Wood. May I, I mean, may I, you know, come over and see you?"

"Eh?"

"I'm longing to see you. May I come over now, right away? I can get a taxi."

"No!" Jeremy blurted, almost shouting. He sensed that Alice, to whom his back was turned, had looked up. Mouthpiece covered, he laughed, "It's amazing the things they do with wood nowadays."

Miss Cox asked, "Is something wrong?"

Jeremy told her quickly, "No no. I agree that we should meet at once. I'll be at your hotel in twenty minutes. Wait for me there."

"Yes, all right."

Jeremy depressed the cradle with a finger—on the second attempt, the first failing because his sweat-slick finger slipped off. Into the dead instrument he said with cackling affability:

"Don't worry, Mr. Green. We'll have this problem sorted out in no time. Good-bye."

As Jeremy turned, heading for the stairs, Alice said, "What a cheek, disturbing you on a Sunday."

"Yes, but he's a big customer. I'll have to go."

"It's a shame, darling. And we've hardly seen anything of each other lately."

"Oh well."

"Tell you what," Alice said brightly. "I'll go with you."

Jeremy came to a stop at the stairfoot. "Er," he said, drawing out the sound like an elastic band.

"Pardon you," Alice said in amused reproof.

He patted his mouth. "I can't take you, dearest. I must see Mr. Green alone."

"Why?"

"Well. That's it. Tough business talk. Might be rough language. Excuse me." He dashed upstairs.

It took him three minutes to dress. It would have taken less had he not stopped the frantic self-wrestling from time to time in order to listen for sounds from below. He was terrified lest Alice insist on going along.

Downstairs, he slipped outside after snapping, "Back soon." He hurried along the street. His fear switched from Alice to Miss Cox. What on earth, he seethed. What on bloody earth. Sex on the brain, that's what. Probably nympho.

Jeremy changed his mind about that. Pride intervened. He grudgingly allowed that all this was his own fault. He should never have used his sophisticated lovemaking on the provincial girl, who had previously been only fumbled with oafishly.

Jeremy was smiling as he turned the corner. His smile drained and he forgot Miss Cox. Standing there was Henry Mastin.

Jeremy drew to an untidy halt. He was shaken. This was as much on account of the state of the other man's person as of his presence here.

Henry Mastin looked sick and forsaken. His clothes were rumpled and dirty, as though they had been slept on by old dogs. His hair was awry. A stubble of beard mottled his fat jowls. He was pale and red in the eye and without expression. Most worrying of all, his tie was loosely knotted.

He said, "Hoped I might see you."

"Fine," Jeremy said, showing half of his top teeth. "Fine, old man."

"Had the feeling you were avoiding me."

"Good heavens, my dear fellow. What an idea."

"Was just about to come to the house."

Jeremy moved forward. "What?"

"Like to talk to you and Alice."

"She's in bed," Jeremy said. "Headache. Terrible migraine. Can't stand the slightest sound." He took Mastin's arm and drew him across the road. "Let's have a stroll on the Heath."

Henry Mastin gave no resistance. He seemed weak. Head down, he walked in a near-totter. He said:

"I don't want to hurt anyone."

"Um—good."

"That's what it boils down to. Someone always gets hurt. Don't like it."

What Jeremy didn't like was this sort of ramble, which had a dangerous ring. Nervous, he asked, "Anything fresh?"

"Where?"

"The police, old man. The investigation."

Mastin shook his head dolefully. "No. We're clean."

Jeremy didn't care for that plural. People, he thought, were always using plurals at him. He said, "You're not under suspicion?"

"No, not a bit. But it's getting me down, you see. That's what I mean. You know what I mean?"

"No."

"Well," Henry Mastin said. "We're not doing the right thing."

Jeremy quavered, "Oh?"

"That's what I mean."

"No."

"We should be doing the right thing. It's getting me down."

Jeremy dropped his arm, feeling that he lacked the strength to continue the grip. He gazed about him dazedly, as if in search of the new Jeremy. He said, "Look here, old man. Now listen to me." And gave up.

Mastin stopped by a tree. Turning, he leaned his back on it. In his present state, the bucolic setting was all wrong, uncomfortable. He would have looked better against the wall of a workhouse. Focussing red eyes on Jeremy, he said:

"If we explained to the police."

"No."

"Tell them it was an accident."

"No."

"It was just a joke, Mona being undressed."

"Oh yes," Jeremy said. "Absolutely."

"That's what I mean. A joke and an accident. I was joking when I dropped the stool. So we should explain it all."

"They wouldn't understand."

"They might. We should talk it over with Alice, and then do it."

"Do it?"

"Confess."

"Mastin. Henry. Old man."

"The truth's bound to come out. And if we tell Alice first, no one'll get hurt."

Jeremy began to talk quickly: "She wouldn't understand either. Not that thing of Mona being undressed. You do. You're a man of the world. Alice wouldn't believe it was a joke. She'd think all kinds of ridiculous things. She'd be hurt. Her life would be ruined. She'd never get over it."

Stopping for breath, Jeremy ran a trembly hand over his face, which had faded as white as the other man's. Like an innocent bride, he was trying to convince himself that none of this horror was true.

"I nearly told Alice the other night," Mastin said. "Yes, very nearly."

Shuddering: "Christ."

"We could go and tell her now."

"In bed. As ill as could be. Doctor. Pills."

"She'd understand."

Jeremy took Mastin's arm, pulled him off the tree, and walked him away. They both moved weakly, swaying.

Fumblingly, speaking in staccato sentences or garbled paragraphs, Jeremy started a dissuasive lecture. There were only two points he could make—Alice's hurt, the police's lack of understanding—so he made them repeatedly, varying the form.

Henry Mastin kept saying either, "Perhaps," or, "Oh, I don't know though."

They walked for an hour. Jeremy was exhausted. He almost fell down with this and his relief when Mastin agreed not to make any final decision for the time being, and then not to do anything without checking with Jeremy first.

They parted. Jeremy loped off toward home. He wanted to be in bed, curled up small.

※※※※※

"You look harassed," Alice said. "Poor darling."

Jeremy nodded absently. He nevertheless noted that Alice was dressed in her best trouser suit, favourite earrings, and newest beads. He felt more jaded than before.

Sagging over to the couch, he let himself slump onto it. He stared at the french windows. Of course, he mused with a lack of conviction, he could always suggest to Henry Mastin that he kill himself. It did wonders for remorse.

Alice asked, "Was he difficult?"

"Bloody."

"Poor darling. I don't know how people can get so worked up over furniture."

Jeremy twisted his face in painful puzzlement. "Furniture?"

"I don't think I like your Mr. Green."

"I don't know any Mr. Greens," Jeremy said, remembering even as he spoke. He was wondering how to get the statement back when there was a rap on the front door.

Alice ruffled herself, saying, "That'll be one of the association."

"Association?" Jeremy echoed, whimpering.

Alice went from sight, moving across the room toward the door. "They said one of them might pop round this morning to show us the new placard."

Jeremy closed his eyes. He tried to concentrate on thinking up a fair reason for going straight to bed.

He heard Alice say, after opening the door: "Why it's—it's Miss Cox, isn't it?"

"Oh," the voice of the Bedford secretary said. "Oh."

"Oooh," Jeremy uttered, the sound wailing out like air pressed from a corpse.

Alice was tinkling in her social voice, "How perfectly delightful. How nice of you to call. Do come in. What a pleasant surprise. Mr. Wood will be so pleased."

Jeremy rose like an arthritic, in little swoops and clenches. His shoulders were high as if to defend his ears against unwanted hearings. He felt like death. Part of his mind toyed with the idea of rushing upstairs. Another part advised him to faint.

Alice was talking about Bedford. She interrupted herself: "But I mustn't rattle on. Jeremy, look who's here."

He tortured himself into making a creaky turn.

Miss Cox, wearing a hat with flowers, was standing in a preflight slant, its aim the door. Although her spectacles were pointed toward Alice, her gaze was fixed on Jeremy. Her face was starkly drawn, like an unfinished sketch.

Smiling, Alice looked back and forth between her husband and the visitor. She said, "Well, isn't this nice."

"I thought," began Miss Cox.

"Drink," Jeremy dumped out.

Alice brought her hands together in a clap that made Miss Cox start. "Of course. The very thing. Sherry." She moved off and went into the kitchen.

The secretary unslanted. She came toward the back of the couch. She said, "I thought."

Jeremy: "I couldn't get away."

"What?"

"Impossible."

Miss Cox said loudly, "Your wife, I mean. What's she doing here?"

Gargoyle-faced, Jeremy brought his hands to the front and waved them about, conducting madly for silence.

"I thought," Miss Cox said, voice unlowered, "that you and Mrs. Wood were estranged."

"Well yes, I know. I know."

"Will she be leaving soon?"

"Ssshh."

"Perhaps she just called in for a friendly drink."

Jeremy increased the length and vehemence of his shush while again semaphoring pianissimo.

Alice came in. Holding a tray with bottle and glasses, she stopped and looked at her husband, who was hissing and waving.

Jeremy chopped off his shush. He also stopped the action of his hands, though they were still aloft. Through Jeremy's head ran a stream of directions: Pretend you were talking of fishing, or weaving, or that you were going to do a handstand, or were stretching a piece of rubber, or had caught a cobweb, or were giving an impersonation of a woman drying her nails, or say you feel like going swimming, or . . .

He didn't know which to choose. Wearily he gave up. For no particular reason, his hands started on a gentle, useless little dance.

"Bloody hell," he said.

His wife looked at Miss Cox. The secretary looked at Alice. They both looked at Jeremy. He parried with a wan smile and looked at his silly hands.

Alice apparently decided that no explanation was forthcoming. She shrugged prettily and went to the coffee table. Pouring sherry, she said, "Do sit down, Miss Cox."

The secretary said stonily, "I've been sitting all morning. Waiting and waiting."

Jeremy let his arms fall. He advised himself to faint.

Alice gave him a glass. She took another around to Miss Cox, beside whom she stood with her own drink. Alice sipped in her company way, like a vicar who daren't show enjoyment, and asked:

"Did you come about business, Miss Cox?"

The secretary droned, "No."

"I see."

"I suppose, Mrs. Wood—if you don't mind still being called that—I suppose you stopped by for some clothes or something."

"Aaah," Jeremy said. He turned the odd sound into a laugh. Alice laughed as well, though looking puzzled.

Miss Cox asked, "What?"

Jeremy: "Family joke."

Alice: "Oh?"

Miss Cox: "It's good that you can still use these things from your past happiness."

There was a knock on the door. "That'll be one of the association," Alice said, moving away. "Excuse me."

Jeremy leaned far forward over the couch. He mouthed to Miss Cox, "It is a reconciliation. We are together again. For good. For ever."

Miss Cox stared back with a bout of furious blinking. It was so fast that Jeremy was quite taken out of himself. He returned when Alice said, "Look who's here."

Standing with her was Mrs. Hendon. The manageress of Wood's Rustic Furniture was dressed in black. The colour slimmed her body. Her head looked larger than ever.

"Hello," Jeremy said.

"Good morning, Mr. Wood," Mrs. Hendon said gauntly. She looked sick.

Alice went off to get a glass. The other two women greeted each other in a glum, distracted way, like rivals hoping to score by pretending ignorance of the rivalry.

Jeremy felt a little reprieved. He asked, "What brings you here, Mrs. Hendon?"

"A small matter pertaining to business, Mr. Wood."

"Did you want to see me *alone?*" he said meaningfully, glancing at Miss Cox.

"I've changed my mind, actually. It can wait until tomorrow."

"Oh."

Alice had brought a glass and filled it. She gave it to Mrs. Hendon, saying, "Well, this is very nice. A regular staff meeting."

Miss Cox said, sadly, "I'm so happy, Mrs. Wood, about you and Mr. Wood."

"Well, yes," Alice mumbled doubtfully.

In a loud voice Jeremy said, "What a lovely day it is."

"But it looks like rain, darling."

"Does it? Well, there you are."

Miss Cox said, "A kiddy or two might help."

Jeremy laughed.

Mrs. Hendon cleared her throat. "That's a charming suit you're wearing, Mrs. Wood," she said. She burst into tears.

The others gaped.

Faint, Jeremy commanded himself. His vision was filled with the weeping Mrs. Hendon.

She stood quietly, one hand at her side, the other holding sherry. Her head was nodding in rhythm with lurching sobs. Tears chased each other down her cheeks.

She said, "The suspense was making me ill. I've been up half the night. It's been the same every night. I couldn't stand it any longer. I had to come and find out."

Alice asked in a strained, high voice, "What is it?"

"It's Mr. Wood. He's been so strange lately, so different toward me. Nothing's the same anymore."

Alice looked at Jeremy. He shook his head to signal mystification.

Mrs. Hendon sobbed, "I feel he's not satisfied with my work. That's the only answer. I do my best, I really do, but somehow I must have failed. I've got to know for certain. I can't go on like this. I must know."

The three spectators began talking. Miss Cox said things like, "There now." Alice said how sure she was that Mrs. Hendon had made a mistake. Jeremy kept repeating, "No."

Alice and Miss Cox went to the side of the older woman, who told them, "It's the suspense, you see. It's making me ill."

"All a mistake, dear."

"There now."

Jeremy said, "Perfectly satisfied. Highly efficient."

Alice and Miss Cox began patting Mrs. Hendon's arms. With every pat from Alice, a blob of sherry jumped up from Mrs. Hendon's glass.

Miss Cox said, "I'm sure Mr. Wood didn't mean it. He's not been himself lately. It was the strain of the separation."

"I try my best," Mrs. Hendon sobbed.

"A raise in pay," Jeremy said. "A pound a week more, starting tomorrow."

Alice and Miss Cox both grinned fiercely and surged, "There!"

Mrs. Hendon went on sobbing, but now with a smile.

"Emotional conflict," Miss Cox explained. "It makes people act strangely."

Alice nodded. "True."

"How you must have suffered as well, Mrs. Wood."

"Oh?"

"To be torn from the side of your loved one."

"I see."

There was a knock on the door.

"That," Alice said unconvincingly, "will be one of the association." She moved away.

Without hope, Jeremy told his two employees, "Well, it was nice of you to call."

Mrs. Hendon said, "It was the not knowing, you see."

"I was upset. It had nothing to do with your work."

"Heart weary," Miss Cox said. She looked at the ceiling, face sad. Jeremy wondered carelessly if she would burst into tears.

He looked along the room—and sagged. Alice had brought in the new arrival. It was Henry Mastin.

Jeremy put his glass of sherry in his pocket.

Ambling forward, Mastin said, "Oh, I don't know though."

Alice began cheerful introductions. Mrs. Hendon sobbed, "Delighted." Miss Cox gave a sad smile. Mastin nodded dourly.

"We *are* having a busy morning," Alice said. "I'll get a glass."

"For half the night," Mrs. Hendon said, pausing to lick a tear from the corner of her grin, "I paced like a caged animal."

Grateful for the cue, Jeremy nodded eagerly. "Caged animal. Years and years behind bars."

Henry Mastin said, "The truth will out." Face dull, he started to circle the couch toward Jeremy. Jeremy went the other way.

"'Tis better to have loved and lost," Miss Cox said, a catch in her voice.

Alice returned, filled a glass, and handed it to Mastin as he passed. He didn't notice. Alice said, "You're welcome."

Jeremy paused by the end of the couch. A hand clutched at his elbow: "We must talk this over with Alice."

Jeremy moved on. He felt like laughing, which he didn't like.

Miss Cox was telling Mrs. Hendon sadly, "I am prepared to stand aside. Those whom God has brought together."

"Exactly," the older woman giggled, the tears still rolling.

Jeremy slid up to the pair. "Too bad you both have to rush off now."

He was ignored. Miss Cox said, "Let us hope that calmer waters are ahead for the Woods." Mrs. Hendon said, "It was the suspense."

Heavy breathing behind Jeremy sent him on. He circled the couch. Alice passed him, coming the other way. They exchanged glassy smiles. Jeremy turned back when he heard:

"Alice, I've got something to tell you."

"Yes, Henry?"

"Biscuits," Jeremy said, grabbing his wife's shoulder. "We must serve our guests some biscuits."

"In a minute, darling. Henry wants to tell me something."

Mastin said, "That's right, Alice. You listen. I know you'll understand."

The french windows opened. Everyone turned.

Mr. Barlow came in. Pausing on the threshold, he lied blandly, "Oh, sorry. I didn't know you had company."

"Come in!" Jeremy shouted. "It's a party. Come in and have a biscuit."

Alice moved away. "I'll get a glass."

Henry Mastin took hold of Jeremy's lapel. "Now look here."

Pulling free, Jeremy strode to Mr. Barlow, linked his arm firmly, and rushed him over to the two women, who put out helping hands when Mr. Barlow, abruptly released, lurched unsteadily.

Mastin came up. Jeremy gabbled names. Everyone jabbered over a tangle of cat's-cradling hands. Alice returned and gave Mr. Barlow an empty glass, saying, "It's sherry."

The six people stood in a tight knot. Hysteria was in the air. Everyone talked and nobody listened. Miss Cox was poetical and melancholy. Mr. Barlow wore the face of fear. Mrs. Hendon was weepily cheerful. Alice looked dazed. Henry Mastin droned glumly. Jeremy was laughing and not liking it.

A booming sound came from the front window. Everyone whirled.

Against the background of a placard that was held upside down, a grinning face had pressed itself grotesquely on the glass.

Miss Cox fainted.

※※※※※

How Jeremy got through Sunday he would never, he told himself, know. The same went for the day after. That, if anything, was worse. At least on Sunday, with Miss Cox recovered and everyone got rid of (Mastin eased out with the rest), he was able to claim a headache and go to bed and curl up small with his twittering nerves. Monday was hell.

Throughout working hours Jeremy had to put on a show of normalcy while suffering his worries. He fretted:

Would Mastin tell Alice? Was he at the house telling her now, this minute? Would it be wise to call Alice and say leave for a week's holiday at once? Would Mastin go to the police? And if so, would he, Jeremy, be charged with being an accomplice? And if all that murder business turned out right, what about Miss Cox? Would she cause trouble—threats, blackmail, a confession to Alice?

Jeremy was shattered. Every time the shop door opened, or Mrs. Hendon spoke, or the telephone rang, or Tom Barr coughed—Jeremy gave a gasping jump.

Between sessions of metaphorically fingering worry-beads, Jeremy bemoaned his paradise lost. Everything was now a mess and total disaster seemed imminent. Before, his life had been perfect and serene. He had owned a wonderful, beautiful wife who knew her place. He had owned freedom. He had owned a sound business now falling apart due to higher wages. He had been so happy.

Mid-afternoon, finding his shoes intolerably tight, Jeremy sent Mrs. Hendon out on an invented errand. He exchanged new shoes for old, plus the six socks. It was a minor anodyne.

At five o'clock he got away and went limply home. Alice kissed his cheek while he fumbled rapidly, "Henrybeenhere?"

"What, darling?"

"Um—any visitors today?"

"No."

"No one? Not one single person?"

"Only Mr. Barlow."

"That's all right."

Alice said, "He was very sweet. He went into raptures about the colour of this miniskirt. Couldn't take his eyes off it."

"Mmm."

"Myself, I don't see anything special about brown."

Jeremy felt easier. However, hardly had they settled to their gin and tonics before Alice started on the subject that had consumed her at breakfast: how odd it had been yesterday.

"Yes," Jeremy said. "What's on telly tonight?"

"I mean, it was just as though everyone was drunk. Crying and laughing and fainting and stuff."

"A bit tight."

"No, darling," Alice said. "Actually, I think I was the only one who even tasted the sherry. Everybody else left it or got rid of it. Poor Miss Cox, she spilled hers when she flaked out."

"She'd had a few before she came."

"Was that it? Well, she was very odd. Kept saying odd things."

"A walk," Jeremy said. "Must take Fifi out."

"Do you know what she said just as she was leaving?"

Halfway up from the couch, Jeremy paused to stare. "No, I don't know."

"I didn't think you did."

"She was terribly drunk, dear. Terribly."

"She said it was to be hoped I'd find it in my heart to forgive you."

Jeremy continued his rise. "Stoned out of her mind. I've advised her to join AA."

"Do finish your drink, darling."

"Later. Fifi first."

Alice asked holdingly, "You did like the placard, didn't you?"

"Oh yes."

"Freedom or Death. It does have a ring to it."

"Very," Jeremy said. "Fifi!"

Outside, he strode quickly until he was on the Heath. His urgency easing, he ambled. He was not, however, relaxed. He doubted if he would ever be able to relax again as long as he lived.

All Jeremy's frets came back to plague him. He turned to Tarzan but found him elusive—the two Simbas and the Umgowa he uttered failed entirely.

At last, telling himself he should be home in case Mastin came or Miss Cox telephoned, he changed course and headed rapidly back.

When passing a trail of low bushes, Jeremy saw the man who had become his enemy. Henry Mastin was fifty yards away. Jeremy dropped to the grass, hidden by the bushes.

Mastin's voice floated plaintively across the Heath. "Wood!" It was a drawn-out call like that of a sick wolf.

Jeremy began to move along on his hands and knees. He went faster when he heard Mastin call again and judged the sound to be closer. His knees hurt.

Looking up, he saw that he had an observer. Tinkle's mother, a woman with a spaniel, stared at him from a safe distance, which she was making safer by taking backwards steps.

To show what a jolly jest it all was, Jeremy formed his mouth into the shape of a laugh, and wagged his head. Then he yelped as he was goosed by Fifi's nose. This introduced to him the horrid possibility of being had sexually by a large shaggy dog with bad breath.

Tinkle's mother turned and strode away.

"I say, Wood!" Mastin called.

Jeremy hurried on. He told himself he couldn't stand it. But he kept going. "Shut up," he hissed to Fifi, who was snapping playfully at his heels.

The line of bushes ended. Jeremy got up and walked. A quick glance back showed him Mastin standing at the spot where he had dropped from view.

"There you are, Wood. I say!"

Jeremy went on. He took long, fast, swooping strides.

Mastin called, "Wait a minute, old man!"

Jeremy realised that giving this impression of outright escape could be fatal. He stopped and turned, shielded his eyes with both hands, swept his gaze around, turned, and went loping on. The whole act had been performed so swiftly that he felt dizzy.

"Wood!"

Jeremy was now at the edge of the Heath. He could see the mouth of Horsetrough Lane. Since it would be a mistake to go home (Mastin was sure to follow), he headed for another street as he left the grass and crossed the road.

Mastin called again. Again Jeremy did the turning-and-scanning routine. Dizzy, he collided with a lamppost. He whimpered and strode on.

From behind came the sound of running. Mastin called, "Woo —hoo—hood!"

Jeremy turned a corner, and another. He reached the main shopping thoroughfare. Looking back, he saw that the coast was clear. He picked up Fifi, dodged across through traffic, went into an alley, and ran again.

Jeremy trundled to a halt. The alley was a dead end.

Hope still flickering, he dove for an open doorway. It led to a room where printing machines were in whirring action, watched over by two youths. Jeremy offered them a series of winks, intended to reassure, as he crossed the room toward another door.

He came out in a stationery shop. An old man with a wing collar stared at him acutely. Jeremy said, "I'll talk it over with my wife. Good afternoon." He went outside.

The next business was a café. Jeremy entered. There were fragile tables, no customers, and a counter complete with sandwiches under glass and a stained-looking girl reading a comic.

Putting Fifi down, Jeremy sat at a table and sagged. He felt three thousand years old.

The door opened. In came Henry Mastin.

※※※※※※※

Jeremy noted blearily that Mastin was less unkempt than previously, though still not his former neat self. He was shaven, his suit had been partially brushed, and the knot of his tie was medium small.

Face wearing a trace of expression, Henry Mastin came to the table and said, "Here you are."

Jeremy looked up. "Tea and toast, waiter."

"What?"

"Please. And some marmalade."

"Now look here, Wood."

Jeremy grimaced in surprise. "You know my name, waiter."

"I'm not a waiter. What's wrong? Don't you know me?"

Jeremy slitted his eyes and craned upward. "Good heavens. It's Frank Jones. How are you, Frank? Good old Frank."

"Mastin, old man. Henry Mastin."

"So you are. Hello, old chap. Sorry about that. Can't see a thing without me glasses."

Mastin said, "But you don't wear glasses."

"Contact lenses, you know."

"Oh."

"Yes," Jeremy said. "Fancy running into you here."

Sitting, Mastin told in a calm voice of seeing Jeremy on the Heath, of shouting, and of following.

Jeremy said, "I *thought* I heard someone calling my name."

"I shouted and shouted."

"It's these new drops I've got in my ears."

"I shouted and shouted, old man. I began to think you were deliberately ignoring me."

"Mastin!"

The waitress came. She left with an order for two coffees.

Jeremy had taken hope from Mastin's appearance and calm. With a cracked attempt at joviality he asked, "How are you doing?"

"Better now."

"Good show."

"It's all settled, you see."

"Eh?"

"My mind," Henry Mastin said. "It's made up."

"Ah."

"I was taking a little celebratory walk on the Heath when I saw you. Thought you might like to know how things stood."

"Things?"

"The situation regarding Mona and me. And you."

Jeremy said, "Don't forget Alice."

"I'm not. I've decided to let you break the news to her."

"I'm not sure I'm with you, old man."

"The police, Wood. I'm going to the police and tell them exactly what happened."

"I don't believe you," Jeremy said, because he didn't.

"Quite true," Mastin said blandly. "You can come with me or not. Suit yourself. I would've phoned you about it but I've been too busy."

Jeremy mumbled, "Really?" He was despondent but not despairing, kept from the ultimate by his disbelief.

Henry Mastin nodded. "I've been setting my house in order, as they say. I've returned library books, paid bills, cleaned the flat. Quite a lot to be done. And there was Rover to see to."

Jeremy frowned "What about Rover?"

"I took him to the vet."

The waitress came, deposited cups, and left.

Jeremy was staring at Mastin, who was blowing his nose and looking at the ceiling. He looked down, stuffed away his handkerchief, and said:

"I wouldn't want Rover to be left alone, you see. I had him put to sleep."

The very core of Jeremy's English heart was pierced. He was profoundly shocked. Now Jeremy believed. He accepted that

Mastin was going to confess. Yet Jeremy did not go forward to despair, he went backwards to determination. He reached a decision. It was a momentous and fantastic decision born of his state of long-term shock. It was reached not through new Jeremy, nor old Jeremy, but infant Jeremy. His rationale was that of a child. He was shattered into sinking to the clenched-fist defence.

Sitting up straight and forceful, Jeremy said, "You are quite right, Mastin. The police should be told. They should have been told in the first place. We were wrong to act as we did."

Henry Mastin blinked brightly. "I'm delighted to hear you say that, old man. You really mean it?"

"I most certainly do."

"And you'll go with me to the police?"

"Yes. We're in this together, Mastin old fellow. Together we'll see it through."

"That's the spirit."

"One for all and all for one."

Henry Mastin stuck out his hand. He and Jeremy shook firmly. "Thank you, Wood."

"Not at all."

"Just a couple of old anarchists, that's us."

"Right."

Mastin tugged on his lapels and began to rise. "Come along then."

Jeremy said, "Oh, I can't go *now*, old man."

"I'll wait till you've finished your coffee."

"No, I mean I can't go this evening."

Henry Mastin sat down. "Why not?"

"We have a couple coming for dinner. But I'll tell you what, if you meet me tomorrow at this time, we'll do it then. Meet me by that high clump of bushes on the Heath."

Mastin looked suspicious and disappointed. "I'd set my heart on doing it tonight."

"This couple we've got coming for dinner," Jeremy said, crafty as a five-year-old, "they're football fans. They want to show me their collection of club badges. I'd hate to let them down."

Mastin squared his shoulders and drove off the suspicion. "I understand."

"So there you are."

"I could still go to the police myself."

"I'm a witness to the fact that it was an accident," Jeremy warned. "You'd better wait till I'm with you."

Mastin sighed. "Oh, all right. Tomorrow then."

In a moment, they left the café and separated. Jeremy went along the street, seeing and hearing nothing. He was working on the details of his decision. How, exactly, was he going to kill Henry Mastin?

SIX

Your demands are unrealistic. I do not have that much money. Furthermore, I do not believe you possess the proof you claim. X.

All right, I accept that you have evidence. But it is not conclusive. Even so, it would put me in an awkward position with the police because of my record. I will pay half of what you ask. X.

Agreed. One first and final payment. Be there alone at seven. I will have the cash with me. X.

These were the three notes Jeremy drafted in his head that same night. He particularly liked the X signature. It had something. Tone.

At length, Alice finally asleep, Jeremy got up to perform his task, in which he foresaw no difficulties.

He tiptoed downstairs carrying a blanket and the typewriter.

The room was lit amply if grimly by a streetlamp filtering past the curtains. Fifi stared from her basket, shivering like a newly guillotined head.

Jeremy, working quietly, uncased the typewriter and set it in the middle of the floor. Next he opened out his blanket. Being neat about corners, he spread it over the typewriter. The covering would make excellent insulation against noise. Satisfied with the incipient tent, he tiptoed into the kitchen.

First, he told himself, gloves. But he couldn't find the rubber pair Alice used for washing dishes. He looked everywhere, shuddering at each drawer-ratch and hinge-squeal.

Finally he was forced to settle on fluffy woollen gloves as thick as toast. He didn't care for the red-and-blue plaid, either.

He stretched them on and looked for paper. That was easy. There was a writing pad with several sheets remaining. He separated three and folded what was left into his pajama pocket.

Clever, he thought. Professional. When the rest of the pad was burned—shop incinerator—there would be no connexion with the notes. Smart. But then, the whole idea was as smart as a whip.

Method had been simple. Jeremy had settled on that within five minutes of his momentous decision. Motive had been more elusive. It had taken him the rest of his two-hour walk to find the answer, which came from recalling one of his fears re Miss Cox.

If the deceased had on his person notes obviously written in answer to blackmail demands, the assumption would be that the victim had chosen murder instead of payment. Should the police think the "evidence" related to Mona Mastin's death, all the better. Someone who has killed once . . .

Smiling slyly, Jeremy picked up the paper, took a flashlight off a shelf, and went back to the living room. He got down on his elbows and knees, folded low, lifted the blanket, and began to crawl underneath it.

His smile soured. He was taking the blanket with him. It trucked along on his back. Retreating, he started again, snuggling even lower while wriggling his shoulders and head.

Still no good. He uncovered himself with a thrust of annoyance—and then gagged with alarm at seeing at close range; a face watching with tilted interest.

"Go away!" Jeremy hissed.

Fifi wagged her tail.

Jeremy pulled a vile face. Its success was aided by his hair being in mad disarray. Fifi drooped tail and ears, turned, and went slowly back to her basket.

Jeremy lay on his back. He pulled the blanket over his head. As well as he could with both hands full, he pushed the blanket down while shuffling along on his spine.

Success. He was covered to the knees by the time he felt the typewriter touch his head. He rolled over. And took the blanket with him. He was surrounded by blanket.

Jeremy moaned. Already the air was stuffy. It caused him to

project a picture of himself slowly suffocating, his cries for help unheard, his legs waving about uselessly.

He got to his knees. From there he managed to stand, and be semifree. The blanket draped about him like a melting bell.

When his panic had faded, he positioned himself above the typewriter. Sinking, he sat on his heels. This was all right. He fumbled on the flashlight.

His three sheets of paper, Jeremy saw, were badly crumpled. They looked more genuine that way, he assured himself.

The flashlight was flat, like a small hip-flask. Jeremy intended to hold it in his mouth, which is what people did in spy novels he'd read.

It wasn't easy. He tried three times before he managed to get it wedged into place. It was highly uncomfortable.

Eyes watering, Jeremy rolled into the typewriter a piece of paper. He had to roll it out again; in with it had gone the dangly little finger of his left glove. The gloves, he suspected, were going to be awkward.

At last he was ready. He began to type. Carefully, using only one finger, he pecked at the first of the messages.

The wool-thickened finger kept bumbling, saliva gathered at the back of his throat, his eyes tingled in the fetid air, he snorted, and his teeth ached. But he finished the note; then the second; then the third.

Exhausted but triumphant, he rose and threw off the blanket, which he had grown to hate. He unburdened his mouth. He licked the taste away while examining the notes.

The wording was perfect. Not actually mentioning the murder of Mona Mastin was a stroke of brilliance. People always put more faith in what they deduced than in what they were told.

Each note Jeremy folded and put in his pocket with the remainder of the writing pad. The flashlight he returned, the blanket he folded (roughly), the typewriter he recased. His crafty smile came back. Motive was set.

As Jeremy went softly upstairs, he assured himself again that the invention of motive had been necessary. It was true that there had been muggings on Hampstead Heath and that Mastin's death could be seen as one. But for a couple to be killed within a fortnight of each other, that was too much of a coincidence. The deaths would be put together, but with no reason the police would be unhappy and start poking around in every direction and at every person who had known the Mastins. Given a motive on a plate, however, the police would go one way and for one type—someone with a criminal record, as per note number two.

After putting the typewriter and blanket where they belonged, in the spare bedroom, Jeremy went into his own room; Alice made no move or murmur even when Jeremy accidentally let the door click.

He went to where a chair wore his jacket, and into its pockets he put first the papers, last the gloves.

He slipped into bed, closed his eyes, and insisted, *I will not think about tomorrow.* He began to think about tomorrow.

※※※※※※

"You're early, Mr. Wood," the manageress said. "Good morning."

But not early enough, Jeremy fumed tiredly. He wished Mrs. Hendon were a little less diligent. He had been hoping to have the place to himself for a few minutes. Now the night before's fifty or so visualisings of scene number one were wasted.

"Good morning," he said, showing a lot of teeth. His hands made their usual abortive catching gesture as Mrs. Hendon leaned forward with a stern nod:

"We're looking a trifle heavy around the eyes, Mr. Wood. If I may say so."

On the whole, Jeremy preferred the flustered Mrs. Hendon to the standard model. He was sorry now about that pound raise. More ruthless, that's what he should be.

He explained meekly, "I sat up late reading. One of those books you can't put down. You know."

"Was it edifying, Mr. Wood?"

"Not really, no. Cowboys."

Mrs. Hendon turned away. "The post has arrived," she said. It was as though she were ordering a child to pull his socks up.

Jeremy lost a good part of his pride. The rest of it went when he saw an envelope marked PERSONAL and postmarked Bedford. He put it in his pocket, got away as soon as he could, and went to the lavatory.

Miss Cox's letter was not blackmail. It was a sweet-sad closing of an account. As full of flourish as the last, it said things about sleeping dogs lying, water under bridges, dead burying their dead, and ill winds. It also said Miss Cox had a date to play bingo with her ex-boyfriend.

Jeremy smiled and breathed in deeply. Not only was the Miss Cox danger over, the fact of its being so was like a good omen.

Jeremy had intended going ahead anyway, but he felt better about it now. He could visualise the final scene with more credibility and less horror.

So there had been no need for last night's replaying of scene number two, the allaying of Tom Barr's suspicion during the use of the incinerator. All to the good. One success . . .

Jeremy tore up Miss Cox's letter and dropped it in the pan. He added the writing pad from his pocket, shredded, and flushed the lot away.

He went out, strode to where Mrs. Hendon sat typing, told her that he found cowboy stories very interesting, enjoyed her wince, turned, and headed out to the back for scene number three.

Tom Barr was washing the van and having an early cough. The latter's noise all but drowned the hiss as a cigarette was covertly dropped into the bucket of water.

"Morning, Tom."

"Morning, sir."

"Washing the van, I see."

"Oh?"

"Make a thorough job of it," Jeremy said. He afted his hands and strolled toward a long workbench. Its top was a jumble of tools. He looked them over as he approached. Not one of them could he remember acquiring.

He stopped by the bench and at once saw the ideal weapon. It could, in fact, be the bar of iron mentioned by the police. It was a tyre lever, two inches broad and twelve long, a mild lip at one end.

The only problem, Jeremy thought, was concealment. Would the lever fit in his inside breast pocket?

He was reaching out when he sensed the lumpy, greasy presence of Tom Barr. Jeremy had a good look at his fingernails, then turned. The ageing youth was weaving to a stop at his side.

"Ah," Jeremy said. "Tom."

"Yes."

"Good morning."

"Morning."

"How's the van?"

"Fine, sir."

"Finished?"

"No."

Jeremy cleared his throat. "Well, make a good job of it, Tom."

"Yes."

Tom Barr made no move to go. He stood on, smiling blankly, his little gaze beamed on an oil can.

Stepping along the bench, Jeremy pretended interest in a coil of wire. Tom Barr followed.

Jeremy said, "I was thinking of taking an inventory."

"Wages," Tom Barr said, wrenching out the word with a twist of his shoulders.

"What?"

"Mrs. Hendon." Pause. "Pound more." Pause. "A week."

"That's right."

Tom Barr looked at the ground. "Same."

"You want a raise?"

"Yes."

"Very well, Tom. You may have a raise. We'll discuss the exact amount later, when you've finished washing the van. Okay?"

Tom Barr nodded. He lost his smile and took on an expression of scared gravity. And he went on standing there.

"Let's agree on a pound, then," Jeremy said. "How's that?"

"Yes. Thanks."

"That's all right."

Tom Barr said, "Me mum said I should ask, see, so I did."

Unsettled by this outpouring, Jeremy snapped, "Good. Now will you please get back to work."

"Yes, sir."

"Fine. Dandy. Great."

Tom Barr said, jaw out, eyes narrowed, "I'll wash the van."

"Do."

"Needs it."

"I know."

Lashed But Not Leashed

Tom Barr took a narrow sighting on the workbench. He asked, "Inventory, eh?"

Jeremy gave up. He knew about loneliness. Folding his arms, he began to chat with Tom Barr, who throughout kept a pack of cigarettes on the move from one pocket to another.

At length Jeremy looked at his watch and said, "Take a ten-minute break, if you like."

Tom Barr left hurriedly.

Moving back along the bench, Jeremy lifted the tyre lever. It was nice and weighty. Furthermore, the shiny surface bore neither trademark nor code number. Probably millions like it, Jeremy thought.

He tried the lever in his pocket. The curled tip made a slight bulge beside the notch of his lapel. It was not perfect, he mused, but it would suffice. And if success went on following success, that would be worrisome. The chain had to break sometime.

Which thought allowed Jeremy to be comforted by the fact that now, when he walked away from the bench, the lever tip clonked rhythmically and painfully against his collar bone. He decided to leave it that way rather than make adjustments.

The day moved along. Whenever Jeremy felt, irritably, that time was going slowly, he would check his watch and see that he was mistaken, which made him feel, breathlessly, that time was going too fast.

Occasionally he twitched.

He sought to keep his mind occupied with customers, and more than once, in heading for newcomers, found himself in a loping race against Mrs. Hendon.

Jeremy left at five o'clock and walked to the Underground station. While queueing for his ticket, he was jostled aside with brute indifference by a camera-clad tourist. Infant Jeremy dissolved; old Jeremy rushed home from the exile ordered by hysteria, and snorted; while new Jeremy lengthened his spine and was about to remonstrate.

Instead, the adults became one and realised the preposterous: that he, Jeremy Wood, was in the process of committing a murder.

He gaped like a hooked fish between struggles. He was unaware of being buffeted by a swarm of commuters.

When he did become so aware, after a particularly heavy jolt, the brief reign of personality change staggered toward its end. The youngster revolted, exulting in the storybook heroics.

Yes, he was going to kill. He was going to destroy the foe.

Jeremy strutted back into line. On the street, he headed for Horsetrough Lane. If he walked with a sway, he discovered, the tyre lever wagged instead of nodded, giving no snaps of pain. He became engrossed in cultivating this walk, unaware of odd looks.

When Jeremy reached home, Alice was on the telephone. The caller, he gathered, was an association member. After exchanging with his wife a kissing sound and pucker, Jeremy went into the kitchen. He mixed two drinks, gin and tonic for Alice, ginless tonic for himself. He wanted to keep a clear head, which he thought pretty shrewd.

The following hour was easier than Jeremy had expected. Alice, he supposed, would return to her dissection of the crazy Sunday. She lacked opportunity. Two more association members called, and there was dinner to prepare; Jeremy maintained a monologue on a garden arch of latticed willow.

Getting out without Fifi, who might prove a nuisance, also passed off with ease. Jeremy merely said, "I shan't bother taking old Fifers with me tonight. See you soon, darling."

Alice, on her way to the kitchen, nodded absently. "Okay, love."

※※※※※※

Jeremy swayed along the street. Surreptitiously he tapped his pockets, as if making a slipshod sign of the cross: lever, letters, gloves. The lack of balance bothered him. He touched his brow: brains.

Soon Jeremy was on the Heath. He felt jittery, as though he were on his way to show his father a devastating report card.

Stopping to look around once the houses were out of sight, Jeremy saw that few people were about: he counted two singles and a couple.

Some one hundred yards ahead stood the high clump of bushes where he had arranged to meet Henry Mastin. It was deserted.

What if he doesn't turn up? Jeremy thought suddenly.

Wouldn't that be just like the traitorous sod. Worse, what if he's already gone to the police?

Jeremy twitched. But then he cautioned himself not to jump to conclusions. It was early yet. And Mastin could well be on the far side of the bushes.

Jeremy put on his gloves. There was doubt in his eyes as he looked at the red-and-blue checks. Something in dark-grey kid was called for. But then, he wasn't wearing a trench coat either, with a bulge under the left armpit.

The bushes looked like green elephants having an orgy. Between bodies were narrow slices of space; underfoot, the ground was worn brown by a thousand games of Indians.

Jeremy thought he could always creep inside and hide until Mastin showed up. It would be better than hanging about in the open and perhaps being seen.

Bolstered, he strode on, rounded the bushes—and saw Henry Mastin. Jeremy felt, denying logic, that it was his arming himself with a precaution that had made the other man appear.

Henry Mastin was still bright and clean and neat. He stood with feet planted firmly.

Raising his eyebrows at the gloves, Mastin said, "Oh?"

"Allergy," Jeremy offered with confidence. "There are certain things I can't touch. I break out in a rash."

"My sister had it. Wore cotton gloves day and night."

"Mine's a rare type. It comes and goes. Here today, gone tomorrow."

"All red and wet?"

"Horrible," Jeremy said. "I wouldn't show it to my worst enemy."

Henry Mastin nodded the subject to a close. Stepping closer, he assumed a different tone to ask, "Have you had it out with Alice about all this?"

"Yes. We discussed the whole thing for hours."

"And?"

"She was very understanding."

Mastin made a wobbly mouth of complacence. "What did I tell you, old man?"

"Right."

"I told you, didn't I?"

"You did."

"That's that then. The way is clear."

"Yes."

Henry Mastin flapped his shoulders as if eager for a wheel. "Well, let's get along to the police."

"In a minute," Jeremy said. "First I want to show you something." He reached into his pocket.

Mastin came another step closer and dropped his voice. "By the way."

Jeremy paused. "Yes?"

"That couple who came to your house last night. The football fans."

"Nice people."

"They were going to show you a collection of club badges, I understand."

"That's right."

Henry Mastin looked plaintive. "Was it," he asked, "a good collection?"

Jeremy, kind, shook his head scornfully. "Awful."

Mastin half closed his eyes as if over a tasty morsel. "Ah."

"Wouldn't surprise me," Jeremy said, "if they're not football fans at all. Not real ones."

"Could be, of course. Yes yes. Could be. You do get these phonies."

"All the time."

Mastin sighed in comfort. "Okay. What're you going to show me?"

But again Jeremy paused. He had heard voices. Another second of listening and he realised that the voices were growing louder.

He said, "Excuse me."

"Eh?"

Henry Mastin blushed. "To be sure," he said stiffly. "Quite."

"Nature calls," Jeremy said, nodding at the bushes.

"Back in a sec."

Jeremy darted to the nearest passageway. He followed the tunnel until he had left strong light behind. He stopped, turned, and waited.

There were two voices, male and female, and young. Jeremy

thought it would probably be the couple he had seen earlier. They drew closer. They were talking about someone called Mrs. Rottenface. It's not really her name, Jeremy told himself, shaking his head and smiling.

Mrs. Rottenface was dirty, ugly, and smelly, as well as being nothing but a greedy old miser. Only last night she—

Jeremy was sorry when the voices chopped off—obviously on account of the couple seeing Mastin. Jeremy wouldn't have minded betting that Mrs. Rottenface was a landlady. He wished he knew what it was she'd done last night.

The voices started again, then grew fainter. To be safe, and so as not to arouse suspicion, Jeremy waited until the air had no sound left.

He stooped back outside. Henry Mastin turned from having been facing politely the other way. He said, "You were going to show me something."

Jeremy put his gloved hand into his pocket. He brought out the three notes, which he fumbled with while saying:

"It's a confession, old man. A statement, rather. I typed it out this afternoon."

"What for?"

"I thought it'd be a good idea if we agreed on procedure. You know, the sequence of events."

"Yes, that's not bad."

"It's among this lot somewhere," Jeremy said. He separated one of the notes and handed it to Mastin. "I think that's the one."

Henry Mastin unfolded the paper, turned it over, turned it around, held it at arm's length. "Um."

Bulbously satisfied at all the fingerprints being laid, Jeremy reached out and took the note back. "No, that's not it. Must be this one. Here."

Mastin repeated the performance. Again, before a reading could be accomplished, Jeremy took the note back and replaced it with the last.

Abruptly, his face became hard. He moved back to Mastin's rear and reached his right hand inside his jacket. He glanced around. There was no one to be seen.

Mastin had got the note unfolded and right way up. He sent it away to arm's length. "Um," he said, and began to read:

"*Agreed. One first and final payment.*" He tutted. "This doesn't sound like it either."

Jeremy drew out the tyre lever. He took a step back, raised his weapon high, moved forward again, and brought it down on Mastin's head.

Henry Mastin straightened with a fast twitch. Slowly, his head went up and back on a stretching neck. The note fell in a gentle flutter.

Jeremy, heart apound, waited. Mastin continued to stand tall and rigid.

Jeremy looked around again. The area was still free of people. He moved backwards. He raised his arm. He stepped forward heavily. He brought the tyre lever down in a mighty swing.

The resulting contact made a crunchy clunking sound and sent a shock along Jeremy's shoulder.

Henry Mastin gave out a grunt. A shudder ran up his body and waggled his head. Ponderously, he began to fall backwards.

For a moment, Jeremy didn't know whether to catch him or move. He moved. He tossed the tyre lever aside as he skipped out of the way.

Mastin went on falling, stiff as a tall drink. He landed on the grass and lay there neat and motionless. His eyes were open. They stared straight up with an expression of outrage.

Jeremy knew he had to be dead.

The silence was slit by a voice. It was calling, approaching.

Crouched like a fiend, Jeremy picked up the fallen note. With the other two he jammed it into Mastin's pocket.

The voice was growing louder.

Jeremy turned and ran.

Ahead was the road; it had houses, traffic, and strollers. Behind lay the Heath; undulating land with many bush clumps and copses between here and the scene of moment.

No one had seen Jeremy running. He had been crafty.

Now he went at a walk toward the road. His lungs were working at double-time, his face was flushed, and his nerves were still jittery. But he felt in charge of himself, was quietly triumphant like a boy making an escape from a robbed orchard.

Jeremy realised he was still wearing the plaid gloves. He stripped them off and rolled them into a ball, which he put in his pocket.

That, he considered, was the last act, the final detail of the audacious project. It was now complete. The time of worry and uncertainty had passed. He was once more a person with a happy present and a future of guaranteed tranquility.

Jeremy did not think about the kill. He would avoid ever doing so. The Henry and Mona Mastin chapter of his life was finished, read, and there was no downturned corner on the last page.

He reached the road, crossed it, and walked along beside the houses. His physical state was back to normal, though his nerves had not yet settled.

Looking at his watch, Jeremy was surprised to see that only twenty minutes had elapsed since he had left the house.

Swift and sure, he mused, tightening his features. Faster than a speeding bullet. The mysterious figure in dark clothing struck with bloodchilling speed and then melted back into the night. Yes.

Jeremy turned into a sidestreet. Walking, he went over in his mind the story that would probably be needed later, following:

"What's that you say, officer? Mastin dead? Killed? I can't believe it."

"I'm afraid it's true, Mr. Wood."

"My God. Any other time I might have been there to save him. I often walk on the Heath, you know, with my little dog. But I decided on a stroll in town."

"That's obvious, sir, since you didn't take the dog with you."

"Quite."

"Had you been going on the Heath, you would have taken the dog. You didn't take the dog, therefore you did not go on the Heath."

"Just so. Perhaps, though, I should tell you of my movements."

"Oh, that won't be necessary, sir."

"I'd like to tell you anyway. For the record."

"As you wish, Mr. Wood."

"Well, I strolled about looking at shop windows and things. Just wandering around aimlessly. I can't remember if I saw anyone I know. I doubt it. Then I went into the Royal George and had a whisky. I chatted to the barmaid. The weather and things like that. Nothing of consequence. Finishing my drink, I melted back into the . . . No, I left the pub and strolled home, arriving there about eight. And that's all I can tell you, officer."

"That's fine, Mr. Wood. Sorry to have troubled you."

"You have your job to do."

"I'm glad you understand, sir. Thank you."

"Not at all. My pleasure."

"Good-bye, sir."

"Good-bye, officer. And good luck."

"Thank you, sir. Good-bye."

Jeremy was sad to see his sympathetic officer go. So he brought him back, this time giving him a withered arm, and went through the exchange again.

It was most satisfying. Meanwhile, there was the other story, which might be needed as soon as he got home, should Alice have been looking for the gloves in his absence.

He would say, "Your what, Alice? Your oven gloves? Why no, Alice, I haven't seen them. Ah, but wait. I remember now. I got them and rolled them into a ball for Fifi to play with. I'll just bend down here behind the couch, Alice, and look underneath. Yes, here are your gloves, Alice."

Simple, Jeremy thought. And clever.

He came to the Royal George. Inside, it was medium-customered. Jeremy went to the counter. One of the two barmaids brought a close-shot of her smile. It had green bits at the sides. Jeremy ordered whisky. It came, he paid, and he said:

"Pleasant evening, miss."

"It is, yes. It's been quite nice lately, hasn't it?"

Thrilled to his toes, which actually tingled, Jeremy said, "It certainly has. One of the best summers for years."

"A delight."

"I've been wandering around aimlessly," he said. "Looking at shop windows and things. That's what I've been doing."

"Oh yes?"

"Better than on the Heath."

"Yes. Excuse me."

Alone, Jeremy sipped his drink and exulted. He owned the touch, all right. He had that extra something special.

Turning, he leaned back on the bar illustriously. He was civil about the other customers as he looked grandly around, allowing that they were probably decent people who led interesting and even dangerous lives.

He hummed, sipped, hummed.

His gaze rested on a table. It was where he had sat with Henry Mastin, where they had got drunk, and where the absurd plan was first hatched.

A man, he thought, will do a lot for the woman he loves.

Jeremy looked into his drink. It was halfway down. There were, he knew, three quiet ways of rendering oneself memorable in an English pub. One, tipping. Two, leaving a drink unfinished. Three, answering back the barkeep as if one were an equal.

The second was best. Jeremy put down his glass and, without a sign of regret, headed for the door. He fancied he heard, but wasn't sure, a sound like a gasp.

As he strolled along the street, Jeremy was delighted at needing to bring back his withered-armed officer in order to make a minor story change. While he was at it, he thought he might as well add a poignant eye patch.

"Finishing my drink—though actually I didn't finish it, now that I come to look back. The flavour was just that slightest bit off. The whisky might have been perfectly all right. But being something of an expert. Well."

"I know exactly what you mean, sir. Exactly."

For another thirty minutes Jeremy strolled. He saw no face he knew, and he didn't care. He was full of confidence.

After a glance at his watch, he headed for home.

Jeremy turned into Horsetrough Lane. It was its usual tranquil self. The street's aspect, however, was more attractive than normal, more welcoming. Jeremy wondered how he could have ever disliked the place. Horsetrough Lane had solidity and charm.

He looked at the cars that were scattered along the kerbs. They were brightly hued and clean, rigidly in the middle price range, meticulously parked.

Jeremy thought it was about time he bought a car. He could take Alice for spins in the country. He liked the idea. It was nice to feel generous.

He noted that among the vehicles stood one that was dowdy. Another factor that set it apart was that it had occupants. A third pricker of interest was the car's position. It was parked outside the Wood house.

Jeremy experienced an itch in the backs of his knees. He kept it from spreading by telling himself that the car could well be unconnected with himself, people often parked there; that the occupants could be more of those Res Ass fanatics, or salesmen, or burglars sizing up the scene, or lost travellers; that the car had broken down or run out of petrol.

He also told himself that even if this was what he suspected, there was no need for alarm. What did it matter if the inevitable questioning happened sooner than later? Better to get it over with.

But it did occur to Jeremy that events had moved at an incredible speed.

The car was faced the other way. Inside were two men. One was bald, the other wore a hat. The bald man held before him a widespread newspaper.

Stopped for a read, Jeremy suggested. Seeing what's on at the theatres. Checking the cricket results. Want to know who's died today. Searching in the help-wanted section, desperate for work. You can't read a paper in a moving car.

Jeremy's itch spread. His hands strayed about his person like pet mice.

He reached the car. Drawing level with the men and the door of his house, he stopped and reached into a pocket for the key. He turned as he heard the car door open.

It was the bald one. He had a long thin face and a tall thin body. His suit was missing a button. Below a baby nose lay a slack mouth with a Hapsburg lip. Both eyes, hard, were uncovered, and there was nothing wrong with his arms.

Folding the newspaper, he tossed it back through the open door onto the seat, where it was patted by the other man. He, young and all bulk, watched dolefully.

Bald asked, "Mr. Jeremiah Wood?"

Jeremy blurted, "I've been to the pictures."

The thin man appeared not to have heard. He produced and flashed briefly a cellophane-coated card. "I'm Detective Inspector Clyde." He directed a shoulder backwards. "Detective Sergeant Waterfield."

"Hello," Jeremy said, voice small, itch large. He was at the beginning of his tether.

"I wonder if we might have a word with you, sir."

"Hello," Jeremy said again.

Detective Inspector Clyde nodded. "Good." He brought out a notebook, flipped it open, and glared at a page. "It concerns a Mr. Henry Mastin."

"Ah."

"The name is known to you, of course."

"Oh yes." Itch itch.

Inspector Clyde accused, "Close friends, I understand."

Struggling, gaining ground, Jeremy scratched his stomach and said, "Not terribly close. More acquaintances, really."

"That's good. In a way. I suppose."

Neither "oh" nor "ah" seemed usable against that enigmatic statement. After rejecting another "hello," Jeremy said, "Nice chap, Mastin. I hardly know him."

Clyde ran a little finger thoroughly across his lip, as if applying salve. "Mr. Wood, I'm sorry to have to inform you that Mr. Henry Mastin is dead."

Jeremy monotoned, "Good heavens."

"He died about an hour ago, while being taken to hospital in an ambulance."

"I am terribly shocked," Jeremy droned.

"Of course."

"Heart attack, no doubt. Overweight."

"He died," the inspector said heavily, "as the result of a blow on the head."

"Oh dear."

"He did not regain consciousness."

"Poor fellow."

"Mr. Henry Mastin has, to put it another way, been murdered. And we are investigating that murder."

"I should think so."

"Therefore I hope you won't mind if we ask you a few questions."

Jeremy made his head perform a shake. It came off badly, droopy and loose. The itch thrived despite his telling himself that everything was perfectly all right. But he wished he didn't have the gloves in his pocket.

"If I may mention it," Detective Inspector Clyde said, "you don't seem awfully surprised to hear of Mr. Mastin's murder."

Jeremy drooped a loose nod. "I am. Very. Terribly. I'm stunned. I'm simply stunned."

"You have been walking on the Heath?"

"The Heath?" Jeremy said, eyebrows puzzled. He made it appear that he had never heard of the place.

"Yes, Mr. Wood. Hampstead Heath. You've been walking there?"

"Why no. No no. The Heath? No."

The gross Clyde lip lengthened to normal in a smile. "Yet your wife said that's where you were going."

"Really? How curious. No, I went for a very aimless wander around town."

"Not on the Heath."

Jeremy scratched his ribs. "No."

"Mrs. Wood was mistaken."

"Quite in error."

"Good," the inspector said. "Very good." He had a mysterious look of satisfaction.

Jeremy said, "Whisky."

"Beg pardon?"

"I had a drink in the Royal George."

Clyde appeared disinterested. He said, "Mr. Henry Mastin, you see, was killed on the Heath. Hence, my concern."

"Royal George."

"Tell me, had Mrs. Wood and the deceased known each other long?"

"Mrs. Wood?"

"Your wife."

"Not long, no. A few weeks. We hardly knew Marsden really."

"Mastin."

"Yes. Hardly knew him at all. And we certainly never met his wife."

"Who," Clyde said, "was also killed, recently."

"What a horrible coincidence."

"Perhaps," the inspector said, heavy of lip again.

Jeremy scratched both buttocks. "I had a whisky and chatted to the barmaid. Royal George."

Clyde looked at his notebook, then asked, "Mrs. Wood and Mr. Henry Mastin were not close?"

"No."

"Strange."

"Oh, I don't know."

Detective Inspector Clyde looked up. "Your wife found the body."

Jeremy stared. His itch stopped. He eked a faint, "What?"

"Your wife was with Mr. Mastin. She tells us she was there because she had followed you to give you some information. Something to do with a Residents Association meeting. Instead, she found Mr. Henry Mastin, dying. She tells us."

"Jesus Christ," Jeremy said.

"Exactly, Mr. Wood."

"Bloody hell."

"Yes."

"Alice found the body."

The inspector said, "A group of people were passing and saw her there. She called out to them for help."

"Poor Alice," Jeremy said. "What a shock." He turned to the door and reached again for his key.

Clyde said, "She's not at home, Mr. Wood."

Jeremy stared at the door. "Oh."

"No."

"Where is she?"

"At the police station."

Jeremy turned slowly. He asked, face and voice slack, "What is my wife doing at the police station?"

Clyde said, "Helping us with our enquiries."

Which innocuous phrase, Jeremy knew, usually meant that the person referred to was unofficially arrested. He felt as numb as a frozen ear. He squeaked: "You're holding Alice?"

Detective Inspector Clyde shook his head, eyes closed the while. "She's volunteered to stay. She's cooperating."

"Cooperating in what?"

"The investigation, Mr. Wood."

"But what's it got to do with Alice?"

Clyde sighed, salved his lip in the middle, checked the notebook, and said neatly, "There was certain evidence found on the corpse and there are certain facts that came to light during the investigation into the death of Mrs. Mona Mastin. There is Mrs. Wood's presence at the murder scene, and the irregularity of her story, so it now seems from what you tell me, of her reason for being there."

"This is ridiculous," Jeremy said, his voice high. "Quite, quite ridiculous. You mean my wife is suspected of having killed Henry Mastin?"

"It is a possibility into which we are looking, Mr. Wood."

"Balls."

"Yes, sir."

"She went there to give me a message."

"You were not going on the Heath."

"But I said I was. Before I left the house I said, I'm going on the Heath, Alice."

"Of course," the inspector murmured. He closed and put away his notebook. "There'll be more questions later, sir. But at the moment there's the matter of the house."

"What about it?"

"Mrs. Wood, who, as I said, is cooperating, has given us permission to search the house. However, the owner of the property, it would seem, is yourself."

"Right."

Clyde said, "So we would like your permission to make a search, Mr. Wood."

"Well, you can't," Jeremy said, for no particular reason. He wasn't thinking of reasons. He was frantically concerned about Alice. "You can forget the house. I want to see my wife and I want to see her *now*."

It was a pleasant little room. Bright chintz hung at the window and covered the couch, there was a carpet of cheerful colouring, and the table and its upright chair were painted blue.

Alice refused to let the room's charm spoil things for her. It was not important, she insisted to herself, that there were no bars across the window and that there was no bunk suspended on chains. Whatever the room looked like, it was undoubtedly in a police station. And that was that.

Alice paced trippingly between the window and the door. She was excited. She had never been so excited in her life, ever, not even on her wedding day. In fact, that day had been pretty grim, what with Mummy crying all over the place, and Jeremy vomiting with nerves, and the minister getting sloshed, and . . .

Alice brought herself back to the tingling now.

Yes, this was the real thing, all right. It was a true, living, throbbing drama. Most important of all, she herself was slap in the middle of it as deep as could be.

Once again had occurred to her the fact of Henry Mastin's death. It came and went like a snatch of song.

Her eyes grew moist. She genuinely felt the loss. However, she told herself that although it was sad, terribly sad, he *had* been all alone in the world, and there were no children or anything, so it could have been worse. He was, in a way, better off. Lucky Henry.

But how really rather odd, she thought. First his wife and then Henry. It was quite obvious that both had been the work of one person, or perhaps a gang. It could have been a vendetta. Revenge for something awful the Mastins had done years ago. Evil figures lurking up out of a misty past. The Mastins might even have been criminals themselves. White-slavers, master forgers, diamond thieves, pickpockets. They could have double-crossed their partners in crime.

Alice shuddered with pleasure.

And it had all been so totally unexpected, she mused.

The telephone had rung five minutes after Jeremy had left on his walk. The caller was the association's keenest member. An emergency meeting was being called at once. Could the Woods come?

Alice had thrown on a cardigan and hurried out. She went as a matter of course onto the Heath, following the path she knew Jeremy usually took. There was no sign of him anywhere. She shouted his name; she walked faster. She rounded a high sprout of bushes—and there saw Henry Mastin.

He was lying on his back. She hustled over and asked if he'd seen Jeremy. He didn't answer, just went on staring up. It was because it was still too light for there to be stars out that she knew something must be wrong. Vaguely hoping it was a broken arm (her slings were much praised), she felt his pulse. There was no murmur. She became alarmed.

Voices had sounded. Alice looked up and saw people, five or six. She waved and called. The people ran across, and then for a while all was confusion.

She had asked and answered questions, there were more people, and voices said, "There's blood on his head," and, "That must be the weapon, don't touch it," and, "Watch her," and, "I'm going to throw up, Fred," and, "Here comes the ambulance."

Next, calm had descended with her arrival in a large room full of desks and policemen who kept getting in one another's way. She was talking with a man, rather stern, who had a bald head and a large lip. He asked a lot of questions about past and present, some of which were odd. A constable came and said that Mr. Mastin had died. She cried a little and told them what a sweet man Henry was and said she would do all she could to help catch the culprit.

Now Alice stepped out her excitement across the annoyingly charming room.

The drama was continuing, she mused. If only Jeremy was here too, so they could share it together. It was almost too much to bear alone.

Her name would be in the newspapers, of course, as well as on everyone's lips. Also photographs. Then she would have to appear at the inquest to give evidence, stand up there in the witness box with thousands of people watching. She might be interviewed on television. She would be besieged by everyone she knew for a firsthand account. She might even be given police protection, if they thought the killer, or gang, wanted her done away with.

Eventually the sleuths would win in their unceasing, tenacious search. Which meant a full-scale trial.

The door was tapped on and pushed open. In came the stout

policewoman who had brought Alice here earlier. She had a jolly face and short tight curls like an Airedale.

"Hello, dear," she said, putting a tray on the table.

Alice bowed. "Good afternoon." She knew very well that under the woman's cheery exterior lay a lot of tenaciousness.

"This is tea. It is alleged."

With small-eyed confidentiality, Alice asked, "How's the investigation going?"

"Lovely, thanks. Now you sit on the couch and have this nice hot drink."

"Well, all right," Alice said, passingly hurt. "I must say, this is terribly sweet of you."

"All part of the service, dear."

"What's that other stuff on the tray, miss?"

"Call me Meg," the policewoman said. "They all do."

"Okay, Meg. And you must call me Alice."

"Righto. That makes us mates, eh, Alice?"

"Oh yes," Alice said happily.

Meg nodded at the tray. "This other stuff, it's for fingerprints. I'll take yours in a bit when you've knocked your tea back."

"Fingerprints. Well now."

"It's just a silly old formality, dear. It's so we can eliminate them from any prints we find elsewhere."

The policewoman sat at the table with a sigh. "I'm tired," she said chattily. "Heavy date last night. Out with the boyfriend."

"That's nice."

Meg giggled. "My husband wouldn't think so—if he knew."

Alice was shocked. "You're married?"

Meg nodded, waggling her left hand. "I don't wear the ring on duty."

"And you've got a boyfriend?"

"'Lover' I suppose is the correct term."

"Oh."

Meg winked. "If the men can do it, why can't the women. I'm sure you feel the same."

"Well . . ."

"Come on, Alice, just between us girls, am I right? What's good enough for the goose, and all that."

"Oh, I don't know, I'm sure."

"But you must have had your little affairs, dear. A pretty thing like you."

Alice shook her head. "No. Never. I don't believe in it."

The policewoman pouted, looking wounded. Alice hurried on, "But that's not to say I condemn it. Not in others. Everyone to his own morality, I say. I do, I always say that. Honest."

Meg seemed mollified. She sniffed. "Nothing wrong with a bit of fun."

"Not in the least."

The policewoman winked again. "I'll bet you're a one for the fun and games too, if the truth was known. You can admit it to old Meg, you know. I'm like the grave."

"As a matter of fact," Alice said. She hesitated, blushing.

Eyes fixed, Meg leaned forward. "Go on, dear. Get it out."

"I don't know if I should."

"Do, Alice. And then I'll tell you about me and Sam in the field last night."

"Well, this wasn't in a field. It was in Harrods. You know. The department store."

"I know. Go on, Alice."

"I was having a coffee, sharing a table the way you sometimes have to do. It was a man, a stranger. We got in conversation, and when it was time for me to go, he picked up my bill and said he wanted to pay it."

"Yes?"

"Well, Meg," Alice said, still faintly red, "*I let him.*"

"What did you do then?"

Alice shrugged. "I've forgotten exactly what I bought that day. Slacks, I think."

"But the man. What about the man?"

"Oh, I never saw him again."

The policewoman leaned back and turned a sour look on the fingerprint set. She obviously, Alice thought, didn't care for these silly old formalities.

Meg asked dully, "No affairs?"

"No. But there you are, my husband doesn't chase other women."

"You're lucky."

"Yes," Alice said, thinking warmly of Jeremy. She was about to ask, careful of her choice of words with this professional, if Mr. Wood had been informed yet of her pertinent whereabouts, when the policewoman said:

"What kind of life did you have in Bedford, dear?"

After a moment's bewilderment at the change in topic, Alice said, "Very nice. I like Bedford."

"I had a mate there years ago. Milly Smith. Maybe you knew her."

Alice shook her head. Sipping the tea, she thought how pleasant it was to have a chat. Pleasant for Meg too. She must get awfully fed up surrounded by gruff men all day.

"Milly had a police record," Meg said.

"Really?"

"Nothing wrong with that, of course. Lots of people get in trouble sometime or another."

"I suppose they do."

"Only natural. It's nothing to be ashamed of."

"No."

Meg said, "Why, I used to go on shoplifting tours myself at one time."

"Good heavens."

"So there you go. We've all been up to a bit of villainy."

"How marvellous," Alice said, "that you've turned out so splendidly. You could have gone on and on, couldn't you."

The policewoman nodded glumly. "You never got up to mischief, dear?"

Alice looked into her tea. "Well," she said, "as a matter of fact there was that one thing. I've never told a living soul about it."

Meg's voice sounded tight. "What thing?"

"Stealing cars, actually."

"Go on, dear. Go on."

"There were six of them altogether. It was bad of me."

"Tell old Meg, Alice."

"Well, that's it, I just stole the cars."

"Did you sell 'em?"

"Oh no," Alice said. "I hid them in the back garden. In a cardboard box."

"In a . . ."

"My brother looked high and low. He was livid. I don't to this day know why I did it. A sort of madness came over me."

Meg's voice now sounded slack. She said a stodgy, "Fingerprints."

※※※※※

The construction of Gothic police stations was a bad habit of which the British had finally broken themselves after World War II. Therefrom, inspired perhaps by the loss of ornate India, architects created buildings as bleakly bland as public lavatories. Although those in search of help were no longer repelled, mothers found the new places useless for threatening children with.

Jeremy had no eyes for the police station. He was aware only of climbing steps and of standing in a lobby. He glanced at without seeing the huddles of whispering people and the bustle of uniforms beyond a counter.

"If you'd care to wait here a minute, sir," Detective Inspector Clyde said. "I'll see if Mrs. Wood's free."

"Free," Jeremy echoed with harsh amusement. "That's rich."

"Available."

"The whole thing is absurd." He had already said this eight times during the drive in the police car. It was beginning to sound silly.

Clyde asked, "Then why not help to prove it by letting me search your house?"

"I want to see my wife."

"It'll only take me a couple of hours to get a warrant."

Jeremy stuck out his chin like a faulted critic. "I want to see my wife."

The inspector left. Presently a constable came, beckoned with swung arm, led Jeremy to a corridor, and said, "Last door to your right, sir."

On the way, Jeremy passed a stout policewoman. She carried a tray and had a headache expression.

The door was called Detention Room A. Jeremy knocked and entered. Alice, on a couch, looked up brightly from wiping her hands with a piece of black-smudged cloth.

She leapt to Jeremy in time with a happy cry of greeting. She embraced and kissed him, bubbled and fussed, drew him to the couch, and pulled him down at her side.

"Are you all right?" he asked.

"Of course, darling, of course. It's all madly exciting. I've got so much to tell you. I don't know where to begin." She knew. Beginning, she chattered like a telex. She patted Jeremy, waved her arms, and shot up to demonstrate actions.

Shock, Jeremy thought, his chest aching with love. She's so bowled over with the shock of it all—finding the body, being accused—that she's not herself. She needs calming.

Jeremy allowed the flow of words to go on to the taking of fingerprints. He started to talk himself. Being deliberately ponderous, he told of his aimless walk in town, his drink, and the meeting with Detective Inspector Clyde.

Alice settled, though she still bubbled. She had the faintly amused manner of a prima ballerina visiting a dancing class. Every statement she received with nodded encouragement.

Soon, Jeremy mused, the reaction would set in. Then she would be despondent. She would need cheering up.

Still talking, Jeremy put his mind to work at producing cheery remarks and items of news. Several occurred to him—the barmaid, the fun of aimless wanders, the oddness of being in town without seeing anyone you knew. None, however, struck the right note. Jeremy had the desire to offer Alice some form of confession. He felt the need to bend a metaphorical knee.

The shoes, he thought. There you are. Perfect. When she had hit the bottom he would say, "It's ridiculous, Alice, but you know those shoes I bought recently?"

"Yes, darling, I most assuredly do."

"Well listen. They're too big for me, Alice. Far too big. I should have let you do the buying, as always."

"Oh well."

"I've been wearing"—pause for self-deriding laugh—"I've been wearing two pairs of socks."

Perfect, Jeremy thought. He nodded, hesitated in his talk, and lost the conversational lead.

Alice was chattering again. She pawed him and poked his bicep and rapped his knee. She smiled. Her eyes were clear.

The dark truth slowly twilighted on Jeremy: Alice was not in a state of shock but merely stimulated by events: ergo, Alice did not realize she was suspected of having killed Henry Mastin.

And Jeremy saw that he himself had not accepted that his wife was actually in danger of being charged with murder. It had been an absurdity. But what if they could prove she did it?

"Alice!" he blurted.

She sighed off. "Yes, love?"

Jeremy took his wife's hands, lowered his voice, and said, "Darling, I think the police may have the idea that you did it."

"Did what?"

"Well. You know. Killed Henry."

First Alice smiled in doubt, next smiled as if intrigued. "Really?"

"Yes, darling."

"Goodness me."

"It could be serious," Jeremy said, but already the absurdity was coming back.

"Oh yes. Very."

"Terribly serious."

Alice straightened. She shook her head wistfully. "They wouldn't be able to think of a reason."

"Let's hope not."

"All right then."

Alice was listless. Jeremy murmured, "You know those shoes I bought recently?"

"Oh, that reminds me, shoes," Alice said, perking. "That nice Meg told me."

"What?"

"They found a footprint under the body. Just one. The ground was pretty hard. It's not even a whole footprint, only the sole."

With a feeling inside like the dry heaves, Jeremy saw himself thrusting forward heavily onto his left leg to deal the second blow. The picture ripped into instant presence the health of Alice's position, the gravity of his own.

He got up. "Must go. Things to do."

"But I haven't told you all the details yet."

"Later, darling. Must go." With Alice clinging along he went to the door. He nodded impatiently at the half-heard instructions for making his own dinner.

"Promise me you'll eat properly," Alice said. "I'm worried about you."

Jeremy fumbled a promise, kissed his wife, and slipped out into the corridor.

There was no one about. At the far end he could hear bustle. Somewhere up there Clyde might be waiting to pounce and question. At this end was an exterior door. Jeremy drew it open and looked out.

There was a yard with cars and a Black Maria. No people. Jeremy went outside. As he sidled past the van he saw written in the dust on its side COPS IS SMELLY. It did nothing for him.

He passed through a gateway, walked with prickly back along an alley, and came to the street. Striding out, he looked around for a taxi. There were none. He began to run. When people stared he looked at his watch, laughed ruefully, and shook his head.

He saw a cab. He waved. The driver waved back.

Another taxi came along. This time Jeremy shouted. The driver swung into the side and stopped.

Fifteen minutes later, the taxi was on Edgware Road. Dusk had settled for a short stay. Lights were growing stronger. A wrought-iron lamp glowed in the window of Wood's Rustic Furniture.

"It's not that shop, driver," Jeremy said, cunning. "It's the pub down on the corner."

Alighting and paying there, he walked back while whistling a chirpy air. At the shop he looked around with swaying casualness before unlocking the door.

He got his old shoes from their drawer and carried the box to the rear. Once changed from new shoes to old, six socks and all, he felt better, like a hot lad with his gloves off.

It took five minutes to get the incinerator going, ten for the new brogues to be eaten by flame, one for Jeremy to scrape from the embers the tiny nails. These, when he had left the shop, he scattered one at a time as he walked, pretending he was trying to flick a cobweb off his hand.

A mile from the shop he got another cab and went home.

Jeremy let Fifi out to fend for herself. In the kitchen, after putting the gloves away, he made himself a sandwich. He gave up on it with the second dry mouthful and mixed a gin-tonic. He was still drinking it when the police arrived.

Detective Inspector Clyde and the eagerness-smoothing Waterfield were accompanied by two uniformed officers, a constable and a sergeant. The last carried a book-sized parcel.

When Jeremy had brought them inside, he was presented by Clyde with a piece of paper.

"Search warrant, Mr. Wood. I told you it wouldn't take long."

Jeremy nodded rawly. "All right. Go ahead. But I don't know what you expect to find."

"We'll see," Clyde said, his bottom lip thick and smug.

During the search of the house's lower part, Jeremy stood at the front window and stared out with pointed disinterest in the proceedings. He stayed there when he heard tramping on the stairs. Glancing aside, he saw that the constable had been left below. Their eyes met. The constable tried a tentative smile. Jeremy turned coldly away, softening not at all.

There were thuds from above. They went on; and on. The lavatory was flushed, and Jeremy stiffened at the impertinence. He told himself he would give them all a piece of his mind. The trenchant phrases to accomplish this dissolved as Jeremy turned at sounds of descent and saw Waterfield carrying the portable typewriter.

Inspector Clyde said, "We'll take your machine along with us, Mr. Wood. We'll give you a receipt."

Not trusting himself to speak, Jeremy shrugged, and then became trustful and asked a quaky, "What for?"

"It's customary. We always give receipts."

"The typewriter."

"It's in connexion with evidence of a special nature."

"Oh."

Detective Inspector Clyde took the book-sized parcel from the sergeant. "Now, sir, may I ask you to place your left shoe against this."

It was a plaster cast with fluffy edges. Clyde flourished it free of the wrapping paper as if it were a plaque to his own bravery.

"What's that all about?" Jeremy pretended.

"Cast of a print found at the murder scene, Mr. Wood."

"The killer's?"

Clyde looked disdainful. "Or someone who passed by earlier."

Jeremy took the cast and set it against his side-lifted shoe. "Too big for me," he said.

"As it was against your other articles of footwear. Also your wife's."

"So that lets her out."

"Hardly, sir," Inspector Clyde said. He took the cast back. "To repeat: someone who passed by earlier."

Jeremy straightened one of his shoulders. "You're not still going ahead with this farce of suspecting my wife."

"Afraid so, Mr. Wood. We're running checks with Scotland Yard and the Bedford police."

"Checks on what?"

"Mrs. Wood's past."

"She doesn't have one. Not one that would interest you people."

"Time will tell."

Jeremy snorted, in a way. He snatched petulantly at the receipt offered by the sergeant.

"And what's more," he said, "you've got no right to use my lavatory."

"We weren't using it, sir. We were emptying the cistern to look inside."

"Oh. Well. Even so."

Clyde brought out his notebook. "If you don't mind, Mr. Wood, we'll get to those questions now."

"I have nothing whatever to tell you," Jeremy said puffily. "Nothing at all. I refuse to answer any questions. You can ask till you're blue in the face."

He added, not sure of its relevance, "I'm a taxpayer."

Eyes on the ceiling, Clyde snapped shut and put away his notebook. He looked down with, "So be it."

Nothing more was said. The policemen went out and Jeremy made a point of closing the door with a snap.

He prowled the room, he drew the curtains, he finished his drink, he called in Fifi and opened a can of dog food, he telephoned the police station.

Alice said she was fine. She had been fetched a lovely dinner except for the peas and if it was all right with him she was going to stay the night, as she wanted to help not only for the sake of Justice but also for Henry.

Jeremy felt too weak to demur. He mumbled sympathetic words.

Sprawling out full length on the couch, he closed his eyes, clenched his fists, and bemoaned his fate. The situation was fantastic. If the police did manage to build a case against Alice, he would of course confess, and would then be in the insane position of having to prove himself guilty, and his only real proof—the shoes—had been destroyed.

Jeremy groaned. He groaned himself to sleep.

SEVEN

The following day was one of comings and goings, of telephone calls, of shock and despair and spurts of elation, of constant belching. A hectic, harrowing day. Jeremy thought it would never end, yet was sorry when it did, when the action stopped, for he was alone again with his worry.

He awoke still on the couch. Fifi was straddling his neck like a heavy-duty boa. Pushing her off with a whimper, he creaked upright and wondered how he could have got so drunk. His head ached and his mouth tasted of black poodle.

Jeremy became even drearier as he remembered the sober truth.

He drank coffee and had another bite of the unfinished sandwich. Without concern he heard the newspaper's plopped arrival; then started as if jabbed by a pin.

It had not occurred to him before, but there would of course be screaming headlines in the press of the nation. MURDER ON HAMPSTEAD HEATH, or BRIDGE PLAYER HELD, or ALICE WOOD SUSPECTED OF HOMICIDE.

Jeremy rushed for the paper, skimmed over a rail strike, an earthquake in California, a mine shaft collapse in Wales, and the two-year prison sentence passed on a man for throwing stones at a cat.

He found it. The item consisted of half an inch at the bottom of the page. A man identified as Mr. Henry Mastin had died of a head wound in Hampstead. The case was being treated as murder. A Mrs. Jeremy Wood was last night assisting the police in their investigation.

Jeremy felt both relieved and offended.

The telephone rang. Belching, Jeremy hurried to the instrument and snatched it to his ear.

"Mrs. Hendon here, Mr. Wood. I've just read this thing in my paper. There's some mistake, of course."

"Yes yes. Ghastly error. All be over soon."

"Is Mastin that strange man who kept wanting to talk to Mrs. Wood when I was there Sunday?"

"Yes. Sly type."

"People like that, they do get murdered, don't they?"

"It was suicide," Jeremy said. "Thanks for calling." He put the telephone down. It rang again. He lifted it to his face with care and gave his number. The caller was a neighbour. She had just read . . .

Jeremy told her it was a ghastly error.

Turning away from the telephone, he saw Mr. Barlow striding with surprising agility across the patio and waving a newspaper overhead. His face bespoke outrage.

Jeremy belched.

Racketing through the french window, Mr. Barlow snapped in accusation, "What's all this then? Eh? What's all this?"

"Ghastly error."

"Who?"

"It's nonsense," Jeremy said wearily. "A mistake."

"Printing mistake?"

"No. The police've got it all wrong. She'll be back soon."

"I should think so," Mr. Barlow said. He brought his arm down. "I should just bloody well think so."

The telephone rang.

Jeremy shrugged and gave a weak smile. He felt like a martyr. It was not a bad feeling, on the whole. He allowed his body to sag a little as he turned away, saying, "Excuse me."

The caller was Miss Cox. She said, "Mr. Wood, I want you to be the first to know that I've read it. I'm appalled. Everyone here at the Bedford branch is appalled. I'm prepared to come to you at once. I'll come now."

"No no, don't bother, it's nothing."

"Nothing?"

Jeremy explained the hideous misunderstanding. Miss Cox

said all would come right in the end, it was a lone lane that had no turning, and where there was a will there was a way.

Jeremy rang off. Mr. Barlow asked, "Who is this bloody Mastin any old how?"

"He came here a couple of times to play cards."

"Oh, that thing. I've seen him."

"We hardly know the man."

"Bloody troublemaker."

There was a knock on the front door. Jeremy said, giving that nice weak smile, "I can't talk now, Mr. Barlow."

The neighbour turned away, raising his newspaper again. He said, a threat, "I'll be back."

Jeremy slumped over to the door. He opened it a crack, and then wider on seeing a vaguely familiar face. It was on a fat woman, looming between a green cloche hat and an orange overcoat.

"Madge Willett," she said fervently. "Assistant secretary of the Horsetrough Lane Residents Association. We've met."

"Hello."

"Bear up, Mr. Wood."

"Oh yes."

Jeremy asked if she would like to come in and sit down.

"No time. Many thanks. Calling an emergency meeting. Ask you one question."

"Yes?"

"This Henry Mastin. On the council, wasn't he?"

"No."

"Knew he was," Madge Willett said deafly. "Dear Alice."

"What?"

"She was all for strong action. Noble girl."

"It's a mistake."

"I want you to know, Mr. Wood, that we're behind her to the hilt."

"She didn't do it, ma'am. She's innocent."

"To . . . the . . . hilt."

"All right then."

The woman smiled evilly. She began to swing her arms forward and back, in unison, while keeping her body still. Jeremy was quite taken with the simianlike act. There was a hint of encouragement in his return smile.

Madge Willett asked, "Know what I said to my sister?"

"No, ma'am."

"I said it not fifteen minutes ago, as I was putting on my hat and coat."

"I see."

Swing-swing went the arms. "I said, 'So end all tyrants.'"

Jeremy whistled. After which, however, he felt it necessary to say a cautionary, "Even so."

"Cudgels are about to be taken up, Mr. Wood. Fear not. I go now to sound the clarion."

"That's very kind of you."

"No, you must bear up," Madge Willett said. Evidently she was an eye-reader. "Spirits high, Mr. Wood?"

"Quite."

With a husky, "Farewell," the woman wheeled and walked off. Jeremy leaned out through the doorway to watch her arms. They had gone back to normal.

The telephone rang.

"Yes?" he asked in mourning.

A woman's voice said, "Listen, Jack, I want you to let me know when the sandwiches arrive."

Jeremy tutted. "You've got the wrong number."

"Oh dear. I'm always doing that."

Hopefully, he said, "This is Jeremy Wood of Hampstead. Near the Heath."

"Well, sorry. Good morning."

Returning the receiver, Jeremy smiled to show himself his good nature. He took up a position in the centre of the room. Arms folded high, he looked expectantly, eagerly, from door to telephone to french windows.

Nothing happened. Jeremy belched. His elevated feeling started to recede. His arms drooped. Despair approached on navvy feet.

A knock sounded out of the greyness.

Hissing through a smile of relief, Jeremy went to the door and flung it wide. The man was tall and young. There was something green about him, like a sapling. The impression of youth was aided by new-looking clothes: raincoat, spotted bow-tie, fedora with the brim turned up at the front.

Jeremy, who liked watching old movies on TV, told himself confidently: Reporter.

"Wilson of the *Star*," the man said with authority, which was weakened by his smile.

Nodding in self-congratulation, Jeremy said, "Hold the front page."

The man looked uncertain. "Oh?"

"How do you do."

"Mr. Jeremy Wood? Husband of Mrs. Jeremy Wood?"

"No."

The smile went. "He's not at home?"

"No, but I can tell you exactly where he's gone."

"I should be very grateful, sir," the reporter said meekly.

Jeremy was disappointed. The fellow wasn't even chain smoking. Coldly, Jeremy gave him the address of the shop, adding, "Mr. Wood's there now."

"Thank you. You don't happen to be a spokesman for the family, do you?"

"No," Jeremy said. "I'm here to fix the washing machine."

The reporter narrowed his eyes. "What make is it?"

"Starflash."

"If it's the hose connexion, I've had the same trouble with ours. It was under guarantee at the time, and I wrote to you people, *twice*, saying that—"

"There's the phone," Jeremy said, grateful for the ringing behind him. "Good-bye."

He closed the reporter out and went to the telephone. A neighbour was on the line about that item in the paper. Jeremy told of the ghastly error, rang off, and dialled the shop.

He instructed Mrs. Hendon to be helpful to a Wilson of the *Star* and any others of his kind, and to say Mr. Wood had gone to the Bedford factory. Mrs. Hendon sounded as if she were nodding hugely. Jeremy was glad to be home. Next he called Bedford and told his manager to send any reporters to the shop.

Plumply satisfied, recovered from his disenchantment with old movies, Jeremy telephoned the police station. They let him talk to Alice. Her sole concern seemed to be for Jeremy's stomach. He lied about eating properly.

Ringing off, he practised swinging his arms in unison.

A shadow flitted past the window. It was either a dwarf or an adult crouching. A moment later, an envelope flipped through the letter slot. Jeremy looked back at the window.

Jeremy crept over to the door. The letter was from a neighbour. It said her thoughts were with the Woods during this the hour of their travail. Jeremy was touched. He headed for the kitchen to put an end to his lie to Alice.

There was a knock on the door.

Humming, Jeremy swung about. He became silent as he prepared a stricken face, which itself faltered as the hope came to him that Madge Willett had returned.

The opened door revealed Detective Inspector Clyde.

※※※※※※※

The telephone rang as soon as they were seated, Jeremy in an easy chair, Clyde on the couch. The policeman had already brought out his notebook.

"It's been ringing all morning," Jeremy said, getting up.

"Yes. Sympathisers."

"No, friends wanting to join me in a good laugh."

Clyde gave the ceiling a languid glance. "I do hope, however, that we're not going to have continual interruptions."

Jeremy shrugged. "What d'you want anyway?"

"I thought you might care to know how the case against your wife stands."

Jeremy went to the telephone and took the receiver off the cradle. Back in his chair, he said, "I'm listening. I'll listen to anything. One of my favourites is *Little Red Riding Hood*." He thought that rather good. He told himself to remember it for Alice.

His eyes doing a glazed Queen Victoria, the inspector said, "You should know, Mr. Wood, first of all, about your wife and the late Henry Mastin."

"Know what?"

"We got this when we took up a line of conjecture that was not followed thoroughly after the death of Mona Mastin. A line that formed a triangle."

Jeremy was envious of that one, even though he didn't know what it meant.

The policeman sighed. He said: "Mr. Wood, I'm sorry to tell you this, but your wife and Henry Mastin were having an affair."

Jeremy laughed. "What nonsense."

"I know how you feel, sir, but it seems to be true."

"You've seen Alice, you've seen Mastin. Really, Inspector. Alice could do better than that if she wanted to play around."

"No accounting for taste," Clyde said. "And no denying evidence."

The inspector stared at his book for a moment, and salved his lip. "We've talked to all Mastin's friends and colleagues. Most were aware that he was involved with a married woman. One knew the name of the street she lived in. One even knew her first name: Alice."

"That's cuckoo," Jeremy said tonelessly. He was remembering Mastin and himself in a pub doorway and the former's, "She and I have been friendly."

Clyde said, "Fortunately for us, he was indiscreet."

"A lying braggart, more likely."

"Do you know, sir, what your wife did on the Thursday nights you spent at Bedford?"

"Yes—nothing. Except over the past month." He paused before adding casually, "She had Mastin in to teach him bridge."

Jeremy was chagrined when the other man failed to react; troubled when he said a calm: "Yes, that fits with what Mrs. Wood told us. The trouble is, Henry Mastin was an excellent bridge player."

"Ah," Jeremy said.

"Mastin has, in fact, won prizes."

"Ah."

The inspector said, "Your wife was not telling you the truth about those visits. And she has been giving us the same lie."

Jeremy clasped his hands together. Every bit helped. "But it's not a lie to her. She believed Mastin was a beginner."

"If so, what was Mastin's point in lying to *her?*"

Jeremy waved his clasp about as if it were on a storm tiller. "Well. Yes. I don't know. Who knows? I don't know."

"I believe I do."

"Funny bloke, Mastin. Maybe he did fancy Alice. Maybe he thought he could get somewhere."

"Possibly. We think, however, that he was somewhere already. That the affair had been going on for months. That they created this bridge story for you in order to make their meetings easier."

"It's a lie!"

Clyde nodded. "I can see you believe that. You're obviously telling the truth, sir."

Jeremy felt pleased, until he realised this was making the case stronger against Alice.

"Another point," the inspector said. "Your wife was seen recently entering number ten Carpet Street. It's known to be a house of assignation. At least, they rent rooms for any period one likes."

"Alice probably has an explanation."

"Yes, and it doesn't wash. She said she went there to a Women's Lib meeting, a guest of a Mrs. Mavis Jones. That lady told me, quite vehemently, that she'd never heard of Carpet Street. She denies the whole thing."

"All this is stupid," Jeremy said tiredly. "My wife wouldn't touch an old bore like Mastin with a barge pole."

"We think otherwise, Mr. Wood. Shall I go on?"

"I suppose so."

The inspector again spent a moment looking at his notebook. "The time came when your wife wanted Henry Mastin to herself. Completely. She wanted, in fact, Mona Mastin out of the way."

Jeremy perked. "Eh?"

"Mrs. Wood went to the flat while Mastin was at a football match. She killed her victim with a tyre iron, which she took away with her, and made the job look like that of a surprised burglar. An old gag that didn't fool us for a minute. She—"

"Hold on!" Jeremy surged. "This is getting outright fantastic. My wife comes across a dying man whom she knows casually, and all of a sudden she's a mass murderer."

Clyde told the ceiling, "There's no need to shout, sir."

Subsiding, Jeremy whispered, "I am not shouting."

"I don't need to tell you any of this. I'll leave if you like."

"No. I might as well hear it."

Detective Inspector Clyde said, "Later, Mastin found evidence that Mrs. Wood had committed the crime. What that evidence was we don't as yet know. In any case, he used it to start blackmailing your wife."

Only just in time, Jeremy recalled that this was something he wasn't supposed to know about. And managed a decent gasp.

"Yes, Mr. Wood. Blackmail. That is absolute fact. Her answering letters to his of extortion were found on his person."

Jeremy gasped again. He also said, "Impossible."

"His letters she probably burned."

Jeremy said "but" several times. He had always thought it effective in books and movies. In real life it sounded foolish. It just wasn't the right kind of word for repetition. He changed to a series of "you means." That was better, but he was glad when the policeman interrupted.

"I'm sorry about all this, Mr. Wood. It's a shock, I know. And there's no doubt about the authorship of those letters we found on Mastin. They were typed on the machine we took from here."

Jeremy felt sick. "You think so?"

"Know so. We have ways of establishing these matters scientifically."

It was what Jeremy had dreaded all along but had refused to think about, like a virgin bride who'd heard it would be a disappointment.

Clyde said, "The rest of it you can probably guess. Mrs. Wood decided not to let herself be financially bled. She arranged to meet Mastin. She waited until you had gone for a walk in town—"

"The Heath. I told her I was going on the Heath."

"—and went to the prearranged spot with her tyre lever. She hit him—twice, the police surgeon says—and then on hearing people approach pretended she had just found him."

"Ridiculous."

"Those two hits, Mr. Wood. That points to a woman more than a man, who, stronger, would have needed only one blow."

Jeremy ruffled himself. "Nonsense."

"It must have been a terrible half hour for your wife, not knowing whether or not she'd been successful."

"Fantastic. Alice wouldn't hurt a fly."

Clyde said, "The very words she used herself."

"You've told her all this?"

"Just prior to my coming here."

"Did she laugh?"

"Almost."

"I'm not surprised."

The inspector put his notebook away. He said, "Mr. Wood, there are aspects of this case we are still working on. One is the origin of the murder weapon. The other is your wife's past."

"That I can vouch for as being totally noncriminal. You'll learn nothing."

"In any event, I must tell you that tomorrow afternoon or evening, after we have presented our case to the director of public prosecutions, your wife will probably be charged with the murder of Henry Mastin."

"I can't believe it."

"It's true, I assure you. And that's my reason for coming here. In a way, it's an unofficial visit. Your wife is not taking this seriously, and somebody should. It's up to you."

"Listen," Jeremy said in desperation. "Alice didn't do it. I know she didn't."

"Can you prove it?"

"Well, no."

"I think we'll have enough proof that she did kill Mastin," the inspector said. He got up.

Jeremy said, "For all you know, *I* might have done it."

"While at the same time having a long chat with Binnie White, barmaid at the Royal George? Hardly, Mr. Wood. Good day."

※※※※※

The afternoon passed in similar fashion to the morning. Pace kept Jeremy semibuoyant, though he returned to nerve-rotting despair during lulls in the action. He belched frequently and told himself Clyde was out of his mind, or bluffing.

Following lunch, which was another bite out of that old sandwich, Jeremy slipped out of the house to walk Fifi and buy an early edition of the evening newspaper. The story had grown to three inches. It was merely an elaboration of the morning item, except for mentioning in the last line that the victim's wife had been murdered recently.

Jeremy hurried back home. He felt safely incognito with his overcoat collar upturned and a red golfing cap pulled well down over his sunglasses.

A woman stood waiting outside the house. She looked as though she might have a riding crop, was tall, and had a face strongly suggestive of a horse. Without preliminaries she charged into speech.

Dazed, Jeremy gathered only that the woman, a German, was distressed about some ponies. He escaped quickly inside with the apology that he had no change.

Over the next two hours Mr. Barlow came across twice to ask for news, his false teeth clamped before and after; there were telephone calls; three more sympathy notes were sneaked through the slot by creeping neighbours.

The telephone rang again. It was Tom Barr. He said so, and then said nothing else. Finally tiring of making conversation against the heavy breathing, Jeremy rang off.

There was a knock on the door. It was a woman in uniform who said she was from the local Red Cross and . . . Jeremy said he had no change.

There was a lull. Jeremy took turns at striding around the room and standing in its centre. He tried his chuckling practise, he tried Tarzan, he tried reliving the Miss Cox seduction. Nothing held him back from the inky pit.

A knock took him at a run to the front door. He found himself facing a delegation from the Horsetrough Lane Residents Association. The ten people were formed in a neat crescent like carol singers.

Madge Willett, depressingly, stood quietly at the rear with face averted and arms at rest.

The spokesman said it had been decided to picket the police station. They would use the old placards, simply changing the word "our" to "her," making Her Human Rights Are Being Trampled On. With the exception of Madge Willett, everyone was breathing heavily.

"I think you're a trifle premature," Jeremy said. "It's too soon yet. But I'll let you know when the time is ripe."

Hate in their eyes, the delegation left. Madge Willett trailed wistfully behind.

Following a flurry of telephone calls, it was the door's turn again. Two untidy men identified themselves as reporters. Being careful not to mention washing machines, Jeremy said he was here to mend a chair and sent the two to join the one he thought of as Scoop Wilson, who, he had heard, was shuffling dismally between Bedford and Edgware Road.

The action went on. A neighbour came with a pork pie, Miss Cox telephoned with a cryptic message about glass houses, and Jeremy finished his sandwich.

Late afternoon he called the police station and asked to talk to Alice. There was a long delay. When she came on the line she sounded subdued.

"Are you all right, love?" Jeremy asked anxiously.

"Not bad. You know."

"They're not bothering you, are they?"

"No, not really. But I wouldn't mind going home now."

"Ask Clyde."

"I did," Alice said flatly. "He told me I can't. I could have before, because I was here of my own volition. Now I'm being held. On suspicion."

"It's ridiculous, darling."

"I know."

The conversation fumbled to a close. Jeremy began to pace. Without self-pretence, he worked on the question of exactly when he would go to the police and confess.

Dusk came. Activity dwindled with the light. Jeremy sank into a gloom to match the night.

He awoke the next morning to a rapping sound. Being awake was a relief, for he had suffered through a series of situation-tragedy dreams interspersed with commercials for steel furniture made by convicts.

Lifting Fifi from his neck, Jeremy went to the french windows in a totter. He felt like something a cat had refused to bring in.

Clawing at curtains and slitting his eyes against the shriek of light, he unlocked the window. He gave a croak of greeting and turned away.

Mr. Barlow came bustling in. He stopped and looked around

dartingly. His beaky face sagged from alert to grim: he could sense the lack of wife.

Mr. Barlow sighed long and deep. He missed Alice. He was lonely for her friendly wave, her cups of tea, and glimpses of her panties.

Jeremy had returned to the couch. He sat with hands to head. Like a priest who unsuccessfully exorcises daily, he looked pale and tired and frustrated.

When Jeremy shook his head in answer to the question of if there was any news, everything shook but his hips.

Mr. Barlow said, "You don't know when she's coming home then?"

"They're holding her on suspicion."

"Buggeration."

"They say she was having an affair with Mastin."

Mr. Barlow seethed himself back to being alert. "What a load of balderdash and bloody poppycock. I saw them meself, through the window. Innocent as lambs."

"Yes? Well, that might come in handy."

Putting his head back sternly, which sent the mouth of his Arran Island into a forward gape, Mr. Barlow asked, "And what are you doing about all this?"

Jeremy shrugged. "Nothing."

"Which lawyer have you seen?"

"No lawyer."

"Great. Fine. We're doing very well, we are. No lawyer?"

"No."

"Bright bloody spark you are," Mr. Barlow said. "Got any money?"

Jeremy looked up. "About three hundred pounds in a current account."

"Is that all?"

"I never bother to save. The money keeps coming in."

"Some people."

"What's money got to do with it anyway?"

"Bright spark," Mr. Barlow said. "I can see I'll have to put a rocket under you, get you off your arse. There's things to be done, lad."

"I suppose."

"Had breakfast yet?"

"Not hungry."

"Ah, but you've never tried my sardine omelet."

Jeremy shuddered. "No."

Mr. Barlow became brisk. He patted himself, pulled the flaps out of his pockets, and closed the Arran Island's mouth.

"First," he said, "food. Next, a phone call to my solicitor. And you, while I'm rattling them pots and pans, you wash yourself and have a shave. You look a right bloody mess."

A bewilderingly swift thirty minutes later, Jeremy was sitting in the reception room of a firm of solicitors. He looked clean and neat. He felt awful. His mouth tasted of fish, egg, and small black dog.

The room was musty-needy. It sank at one corner. The framed photographs were yellow and spotted like an old man's hands, and didn't quite hide the patches of damp they were positioned over. The room was as vital as stale food.

Jeremy didn't know what he was doing here. He saw no point in the venture. Furthermore, he had no faith in a firm that had thirteen names in its title, and he had said as much to Mr. Barlow.

"Don't be such a bloody defeatist," Mr. Barlow had said, pointing the frying pan. "Besides, if you don't go through with this I'll thicken your ear."

Jeremy stared at the tabled magazines and gave his resentment to the impossibility of squeezing thirteen people into such a small house.

A man entered. He was well past retirement age and had a heavy limp.

The old man raised a trembly hand to indicate a door. "Mr. Pleasance will see you now, sir."

Jeremy, feeling put upon, went into a first cousin of the reception room. It looked like the garage sale of a bookworm hoarder. Documents were piled on the desk as thick and tortuous as legalese.

The occupant was a small man. Threatening to be plump anytime soon, he had a monastic head of pinkness and fringe, a spinster nose, and the wide-smiling mouth of a useless swindler.

Brown puppy eyes poured willingness from under hairless ridges. His suit was patchy with cigarette ash.

"How do you do, Mr. Wood."

"How do you do, Mr. Pleasance."

They shook hands. Pleasance continued the grip in order to steer Jeremy around and backwards and into a chair. He asked:

"Coffee, Mr. Wood? Cigarette? Anything at all?"

"I'm fine, thank you."

"So much to do," he said, shifting a pile of folders from left to right. "An incredible amount of work."

"It was good of you to see me at such short notice."

"Incredible amount."

"I won't keep you long. Five minutes."

Pleasance waved a flat hand like someone cleaning a window. "But at least I'm organised. That's the secret, you know, Mr. Wood. Organisation."

"Yes."

Pleasance sat down. After lighting a cigarette he said, still with that broad smile, "Tell me about your murder, please."

"The wife's, actually."

"Of course. Tell me all."

Jeremy gave the story as it was seen by Detective Inspector Clyde. He softened none of the facts, pausing only when so instructed by the solicitor's, "Wait, wait."

Pleasance was making notes. He scribbled with one hand and with the other stroked down his front fringe. After each pause he said eagerly, "Yes, go on. Lovely."

Jeremy concluded.

The solicitor stood up. He threw down his pen with a flourish. Smiling, he breathed deeply. The pile of folders he picked up and put down again.

"Mr. Wood?"

"Yes, Mr. Pleasance?"

"I, sir, shall take your case."

"Thank you very much."

"I shall prepare a magnificent brief," Pleasance said, looking plumper. "We shall have to go over the metaphorical ground in much greater detail, of course. And we shall have to choose our man with care."

"Um—man?"

"Our lawyer. The barrister who will represent your wife in court."

"I see."

"A queen's counsel, naturally."

"Oh yes," Jeremy said without interest. He was sure it would never come to that. Alice would never be tried in court. But for the time being it didn't hurt to keep up pretences.

The solicitor was gazing into the distance in the direction of Lincoln's Inn. He nuzzled his thumb against his fingerpads while musing aloud:

"Would Hart-Robinson be our man? Mmm, perhaps. An amusing little style. Light. Gets to the jury. Not too strong. Good year at Oxford. Lifts the spirits of his clients. Yes."

"I'll leave it to you," Jeremy said.

Pleasance licked his lips. "Or there's Peterson Blake Clowesworthy. A trifle heavier. Not to everyone's taste. A bit rough at the edges. But full-bodied and hearty, and admirably suited for the more yeomanlike juryman."

He looked at Jeremy with joyful sternness. "You see how careful we have to be."

"Yes."

"One's brief, frankly, is not all that important. It's the man who matters. Give a good man a bag of half-truths and he'll beat a mountain of facts. For instance, there was Ronson Curtib—for the Crown in the good old days—he got the noose for dozens just by sneezing in the right places. Marvellous upstager."

"I see."

"And Sir Willy Fortesque, KC, he was a wonder with the tears. Used to cry all over the courtroom. Defended the dregs of Soho and never lost a case."

"Good," Jeremy said with a faint hint of question.

"Come to think of it, young Parkerson isn't a bad crier. He could do splendid things with a female client. Dress her in black, hair in a bun, make-up shadows under the eyes. Yes, I shall have to give serious thought to young Parkerson."

Pleasance came around his desk. Stopping, he tilted his head to ask:

"By the way, Mr. Wood, how are you fixed wallet-wise?"

"I beg your pardon?"

"Money, Mr. Wood. Are you financially sound?"

Jeremy said, "I've got three hundred pounds in the bank."

With no change in manner, the solicitor turned and went back around his desk. Speaking as if to himself, he said, "Still, he comes recommended by Jim Barlow, friend and client."

Jeremy got up. "I realise it's not enough money, Mr. Pleasance. So I'll be running along now."

"Tut-tut, Mr. Wood. Tut-tut. Pray be seated."

"Okay."

Pleasance lit a cigarette. From his standing position he glanced at his notes and said, "Having carefully gone over the facts of the affair, it is quite clear to me that you don't need a barrister."

"Ah."

"A complete waste of time, Mr. Wood. The police, patently, have no case."

"Really?"

"And truly. They'd be insane to go into a courtroom with this lot. They might, however, unless we make them see the folly of their ways. You follow?"

Jeremy didn't. He said, "Yes."

"Fortunately, I know the very man for the job. Charley Pole. He's done commissions before for the firm, has Charley, and is extremely reliable. In addition, his fees are sane."

"That's nice."

"And discreet? My goodness me yes."

"Fine."

The solicitor asked, "Shall we therefore agree on Mr. Pole?"

"He's—um—?"

"He's a private detective, Mr. Wood."

"Oh," Jeremy said. He lied, "I thought so."

Pleasance stroked down his front fringe and tapped ash on the folders. "You may leave the matter safely in my hands. I'll take care of everything. You go home and relax."

"Thank you."

"Just one question," the solicitor said. "About your wife."

"Yes?"

"Is she innocent?"

Jeremy nodded as he rose, which felt peculiar. "Oh very. Yes. Terribly."

"Good show," Pleasance said. "That's all. Off you go."

"Many thanks."

"The game's afoot, Mr. Wood!"

****

Jeremy walked along the High Street. He felt no better for his visit to Pleasance. On the other hand, he felt no worse.

Soon, inevitably, he turned to the detective who sounded like a fishmonger. Charley Pole's employment, Jeremy thought, would, if nothing else, show the police how much faith husband had in wife's innocence, might actually result in definite proof of that, and could even produce evidence that husband could use in proving himself guilty, should that be necessary, and should it not, then Charley Pole would of course give such evidence only to his employer, not the police.

The byways of which cogitation made Jeremy's head ache. He decided to stop thinking.

Hands clasped behind, he strolled mindlessly for several seconds.

What, he mused, would happen if Charley Pole were somehow to prove conclusively that Alice had killed Mastin? Well, what would happen is . . .

Jeremy didn't know what would happen. His spirits sank, and his walk became a trudge. He found it hard to imagine ever regaining his vitality.

He pictured himself going on like this for years, wandering around, a shambling unkempt outcast, perhaps a drunkard to boot, a pathetic figure racked with guilt and remorse. His business has gone, his home has been sold, he lives in derelict buildings. People laugh and point when he goes by.

Warming mournfully to the vision, Jeremy sped on across the years via leaves flipping from a calender. He saw himself, white-haired now, standing in the rain outside a prison gate. He has made a sad attempt to render his person respectable. But alas, he cannot hide the decay of soul which has accompanied him on this journey called life.

Seedily to his rear waits a small dog, grey with age.

The gate opens. Out comes a little old lady, hobbling on two sticks. Her pale face is lined by time and sorrow, her eyes are dark-ringed from a thousand sleepless nights, and her body is bent with prison labour. She has asthma. And rheumatism. And dark glasses and palsy and bits of cotton in her ears.

She and the waiting man move slowly toward each other, their thin arms outstretched. . . .

Jeremy lifted a covert hand to flick the tear from his cheek. He blinked, sniffed, and coughed.

Silly, he thought. Stupid. It would never come even to the beginning of that. He'd get a gun. He'd burst into the police station. He'd drag Alice out of there, gun spitting fire. They'd escape in a fast car. They'd skip the country.

This brought Jeremy upright and sustained him for the next five minutes.

He sank again into gloom.

At a kiosk he bought a newspaper. He had no need to search for the item of personal import. It sprang at him by way of two photographs. One was of his house, the other of his wife.

The smudged head-and-shoulders picture of Alice puzzled him until he realised that it had been taken from a group shot of the Horsetrough Lane Residents Association. The accompanying story offered nothing new, except that a police spokesman said an announcement would be made shortly.

Jeremy threw the paper away and went home.

He drew front and rear curtains, took the telephone off its hook, and made coffee. Incognito, he thought, that was the way. He didn't want to see anyone or hear from anyone, especially Mr. Charley Pole.

By making slight changes in the position of furniture, Jeremy was able to walk an undetouring circle around the room. This is how he spent most of the morning. He thought mournfully of his happy past, and spitefully of the unknown neighbour who had given the reporters the group photograph.

Once he put the telephone back on its cradle. It rang almost immediately, making his hands dither. A man identified himself as one of Alice's bridge acquaintances. After mumbling through a sentence of sympathy at the speed of a Hail Mary, he slowed and began to whine about the partner he had drawn last night.

Coldly and devastatingly, Jeremy said, "I don't play whist."

He dialled the police station, asked for Alice, and was told that she was not available. He left the receiver off and went back to pacing. Once somebody knocked at the door. He didn't answer.

At lunchtime, after slipping Fifi out into the street, Jeremy made a sandwich, prepared tea, and cut a slice of pork pie. He ate with a heartiness of which he was ashamed. He ate blushing.

Fifi was hissingly urged back inside, fed from a can, and sat firmly on her bed—earlier, she had tended to trail behind her master on his circling, causing him to look back to make sure she was there, that he wasn't imagining he was being followed.

Jeremy again began to walk. With determination, he kept his mind on the subject of the group photograph. Who was guilty? He adzed prospects down to the three people he had never liked anyway.

Suddenly, he was exhausted. He felt he couldn't stand another minute. He realised how badly he must have slept the past two nights. Lingering with droopy eyelids onto the couch, he told himself he would rest for half an hour; no more.

The next second, it seemed, he was waking up in a dusk-dim room to a loud knocking on the front door.

※※※※※※

Jeremy got up. He switched on the lights and, as an afterthought, corrected the telephone. He hacked off a large yawn. The knocking was still going on. Behind it he could hear voices. They sounded boisterous.

Jeremy went to the door and drew it wide. Outside stood four people. There was Pleasance the solicitor, there was Mr. Barlow, there was a tall stranger—and there was Alice.

Jeremy rubbed his eyes. When, later, he was told that he had done this, he denied it with scorn. But he did. He rubbed his eyes and then gaped.

The three men were laughing and flushed of face. Alice, in the forefront, was smiling quietly. She looked tired.

Mr. Barlow pushed her forward. She came inside and into her husband's stunned embrace. Jeremy fumbled kisses onto Alice's brow while trying to hear her murmurs under the assault of laughing talk from the three men, who had come in and formed a ring of support.

The solicitor's voice broke through. "It's finished!" he called. "All finished!"

Jeremy stared at him over Alice's shoulder. "I don't understand."

His companions winding down to chortles, Pleasance said, "It's all finished and done with, Mr. Wood. Concluded and closed. Your dear wifeling is free." He hiccoughed.

Mr. Barlow slapped his back and swayed. His teeth clicked loudly as he cried, "That's my old Pukey Pleasance."

"Free," Jeremy said.

He was torn jovially away from Alice and introduced to "Charley Pole, the boy who did the trick." He shook hands with the tall man and told him, "Free."

"That's right. How do you do."

"How do you do. Free."

"Precisely."

"A thousand thanks."

"All in a day's labour," Charley Pole said, grinning airily.

About forty, the detective looked like an illiterate boxer. He had a broad, brow-shy face and a crew-cut. His nose took up most of the face space; its flat bridge made him appear cross-eyed, and its flatter base nearly touched the lips of pastry puffiness.

"Drinks!" the solicitor said. "The flowing cup!"

Moving backwards with his arms out, as if towing a red carpet into place, Mr. Barlow said, all host, "Come in, lads, come in. Make yourselves at home."

As the other two visitors followed, Alice told Jeremy, "I'm going straight upstairs. I'll see you later. They'll give you all the details."

"You're really free? The farce is over?"

She nodded. "Yes. See you soon."

In a minute, Jeremy, still mopy with sleep and the surprise of it all, was sitting on the edge of the easy chair, facing the couch. There sprawled the visitors, Pleasance in the middle. Each had a glass and part-time possession of a bottle of whisky.

The three men chattered and laughed and nudged one another. Charley Pole had a minced, precious accent like a mimic who goes too far. Coming from that battered face, it was as probable as caviar with baked beans.

Jeremy coughed politely into a curled hand. This granted him the others' attention. They smiled upon him benevolently, though with that hint of condescension reserved for the outsider.

Pleasance said, "We tried to telephone you, my dear Mr. Wood, when it was all over. The line was engaged. So we called Jim Barlow, friend and client, to help us escort the lady home. A bit of pomp was called for, after all."

Mr. Barlow grinned lopsidedly. "But first we had a drink or two."

The solicitor: "Or three, or four."

Jeremy nodded approval from face to face. He did not, as he normally did when sober in company with the tight, feel that he had done something wrong. He was beginning to be happy.

Mr. Barlow said, "Tell the lad, Pukey. Don't keep him in suspenders." He wheezed painfully at his wit.

Pleasance brought from a pocket a slab of untidy papers, paper-clipped, which he tossed onto the coffee table.

"There you are, Mr. Wood. Photocopies of today's twaddle. A little pile of gold. Dug up for us by the admirable Charles M. Pole and his operatives."

"Well done," Jeremy told the detective.

He said, "Yes, it was rather."

Pleasance raised a nearly plump forefinger. "Item. Statements taken from two of Henry Mastin's acquaintances and six of his business colleagues. Essence, which said gentlemen would be willing to reiterate in court: Henry Mastin was continually bragging about female conquests, which stories were to be taken with half a salt mine."

"Apparently, it was a case of protesting too much," the private detective said mincingly.

Pleasance forefingered another, "Item. Statement taken from James Barlow, esk, to the effect—"

"I said," Mr. Barlow interrupted, "that I'd watched Alice and Mastin together here. Watched through the window for three Thursdays in a row. Before that I'd never seen the man."

"Troublemaker," the solicitor said.

"And each time when I saw Mastin leave I came over and had a cup of tea with Alice. If those two were having an affair, I'm Chi-bloody-nese."

For something to say, to assert himself, Jeremy asked, "So you watched and came over, eh?"

"No, but I *could* have," Mr. Barlow said. "And I'm ready to swear my life away that I did."

The solicitor cleared his throat raucously, as if hoping the noise would flash back and drown out the perjurer's words. He said:

"Item. Statement from a typewriter expert to the effect that the blackmail reply notes could have been typed on almost any Horton portable, of which some eight thousand were sold in the greater London area. I got a photocopy of the notes from the police, incidentally. Old Clyde was quite amenable."

Charley Pole said, "Furthermore, our expert says there should be deterioration of blackness in the typing if the notes were written some time apart. There is not. The chappy thinks they were typed on the same session. Therefore, possibly phony. A red herring."

His head unsteady, Mr. Barlow said, "Don't forget Carpet Street."

"Mrs. Mavis Jones," the private detective said on a nod. "Delightful lady. Charming bosom. She admitted the truth of her rendezvous with Mrs. Wood at ten Carpet Street when informed of the gravity of the situation. It was a semisecret meeting."

"Women's Liberation," Pleasance said. "Bless it."

"*Wives*, old chappy. There's a difference. Mavis Jones of the bosom requests her statement be confidential. She has no wish for a second broken jaw."

Mr. Barlow said, "Does 'em no harm, the odd belt."

"Item," the solicitor said, again poking air. "That meeting of residents which your dear lady chased after you to tell you about. It was quite genuine, as the police themselves had ascertained."

Charley Pole said, "What they hadn't gone into, the silly things, was that she'd been informed of it only five minutes earlier. She couldn't have arranged that. And without it, how was she going to explain her trip out to meet Mastin?"

"Good point," Mr. Barlow said. He grabbed for the bottle.

All three men topped up their glasses, doing so with jolly banter. No one, apparently, thought to offer a drink to Jeremy.

He didn't mind. Haze clearing now, his happiness was coming into place. He clasped both arms around his knees and hugged himself up small.

Alice is free, he jubilated. Alice is free.

Pleasance, after taking a considerable draft, said, "We come at last to the piece de resistance. The nugget of our effort, as it were. Your effort, I should say, Pole."

The detective bowed untidily. "One is forced to agree."

"Item. Another statement backable up in a court of law. Taken from Mrs. Amelia Margate, sister of Mona Mastin, therefore sister-in-law of our Henry."

"Clever thinking," Mr. Barlow said. He left his lips out of it.

"Mrs. Amelia Margate," the solicitor went on, "states emphatically that Henry Mastin was, pause for effect, was impotent. *Impotent!*"

The strength of this news pushed Jeremy into a backwards lean. He nearly overbalanced. Saved by swift, jerking action of head and feet, he steadied himself and said, "Well well."

"Well well, indeed, Mr. Wood. A marvellous, staggering piece of evidence. A clincher, as they say."

Mr. Barlow said, "It could even be true."

The solicitor ignored him. "Yes," he said, sighing, "a bit of beautiful business, which, like the others, has been wasted."

Jeremy chippered, "Wasted?"

"In a sense. They've served their purpose, true, but how much better they could have done. What a dazzle of public glory they could have enjoyed."

"There there," the detective said. "Don't take on."

Pleasance shook his head and sighed again. "If only you had been loaded, Mr. Wood. *Then* we could have gone to work. Oh my yes. We would have dribbled out our evidence piecemeal in court, spacing each revelation nicely to make the trial last and build up fees, padding away madly with nonsense such as character witnesses—while simultaneously demolishing the prosecution's case, of course."

The solicitor looked dreamily into his glass, briefly sad.

Charley Pole said, "Lolly being short, we went instead to the coppers with our facts. We had rather a long natter with Clyde. Then we all trooped off to the director of public prosecutions. Result, release of Mrs. Alice Wood."

Jeremy asked, "And there'll be nothing further as far as she's concerned?"

"Nothing. Nothing nothing nothing."

Mr. Barlow, eyes closed, sang, *"There's an old mill by the stream, Nellie Dean."*

Jeremy: "And the real killer?"

Pleasance said, "They've gone over to their man-Friday clue. The footprint. They're looking for a tall, fairly heavy man. I suggested old Pole here. He was not amused."

"Where we used to sit and dream, Nellie Dean."

Jeremy offered his hands. "Then it's all over."

"Yes, Mr. Wood. Over and done. There's nothing to do now but celebrate. Where's that bottle?"

The visitors stayed for another half hour. They laughed and drank and performed party pieces. Mr. Barlow sang "Show Me the Way to Go Home," "Ramona," and a tearful "Alice Blue Gown." The solicitor demonstrated how he could rub his stomach while patting his head.

Assuring one another repeatedly despite lack of disagreement that they would continue at the nearest pub, the men caromed out to the street. Pleasance, in the rear, told Jeremy:

"Item, Mr. Wood. Your bill for services rendered. It's attached to those papers. It includes Pole's fees. But there's no hurry for a day or two. No hurry."

Alone, Jeremy looked at the bill. He was not surprised to see that it was for two hundred and ninety-eight pounds. He liked that touch. Two ninety-nine would have been crudely obvious. Ninety-eight took the edge off it.

He put the dead bottle away, stacked glasses, switched out the lights, and went happily upstairs.

────

Jeremy paused on the threshold of the bedroom, which was illuminated softly from streetlamps. It was silent. It was quite silent. It was extremely silent.

Jeremy felt a tickle of uneasiness. He wiped it off.

Alice formed a motionless mound down one side of their bed. Too bad she was asleep, Jeremy thought. They had so much to talk about.

He changed to his pajamas, got into bed gently, and lay on his back. Alice, lying on her side, was faced the other way. She spoke when Jeremy had settled. In a low, calm tone she said:

"I'm awake."

Jeremy asked sympathetically, "Can't drop off, dear?"

"I haven't been trying."

"Oh?"

"I've been waiting for you to come up."

Jeremy thought: Why not with the light on? Why not eagerly? He said, "That's sweet of you, darling."

"No. I mean I wanted to talk to you."

"Of course."

"Just for a little while," Alice said. Her voice was without animation.

"Yes, but you sound tired. You can tell me all about your ordeal tomorrow. You should sleep now."

"I'm all right. And there's nothing to tell really. I don't want to chat. I want to tell you something."

That tickle of uneasiness was back. Jeremy said, "All right, darling."

"Listen carefully."

"Yes, love."

There was a pause. Alice shifted slightly. Jeremy stared at the shadows on the ceiling and didn't even try to make them into faces. His uneasiness grew as the pause went on.

At last Alice punctured the silence. Voice still low and almost a monotone, she said, "I know, Jeremy."

"Mmm?"

"Jeremy, I *know*."

He experienced a quiet fear, like seeing a dentist's shingle. Tension began in his ankles. "You know what, love?"

"Henry Mastin," Alice said. "I know you killed him."

It came out so flatly that for a moment Jeremy was unable to drink it in. Next, he gulped, and the tension clicked into being over his whole body.

He blurted, "Alice, that's the most—"
"No. Please. Let me talk."
"Alice."
"Will you let me talk?"
"Well."
"I've got to get this out. You just listen. All right?"
Jeremy clenched his fists and held his tension. "Okay."
"It's quite clear what happened," Alice said. "How it came about. It was because of that rumour of Henry and me having an affair. You picked it up, just as Inspector Clyde did. And like him, you believed it. The idea was ridiculous, but you believed it. That was the reason for your odd behaviour lately.

"Mona Mastin's death, of course, that doesn't come into it. The police were simply trying to tidy everything up at one go. It's only Henry we're concerned with."

Jeremy pretended an improvised, "I don't understand any of this."

"Yes you do. Please listen. It's all very simple, motive and method."

"Royal George. Barmaid."

"You went there afterwards. Don't keep interrupting, please."

Jeremy whispered, "Sorry."

"So you decided to kill the man you thought was my lover," Alice said. "You planned it carefully. Trying to make it look like blackmail was clever, also the line about the writer having a police record. The notes you typed on our machine, of course. You did that when I was out somewhere."

Despite his fear and tension, Jeremy was able to sense in Alice what seemed like enjoyment, a heroinelike appreciation of the terrible situation she had got herself into.

"You bought a tyre lever," Alice said. "In a busy shop and wearing a disguise. A false beard, I imagine. Also, you bought a pair of gloves. You left Fifi at home on the fateful night, went to meet Henry, and struck him a mortal blow. You ran away when you heard me coming—and I vaguely remember hearing that, the sound of hasty exit.

"After pushing the gloves down a drain, you went for a drink to establish an alibi. Then you went home. It's all quite clear."

"Alice," Jeremy tried, "there's the footprint."

"It could have been there for days, Jeremy. No, it all fits. I've been thinking about it throughout the day. There's no doubt in my mind. You killed Henry Mastin."

Jeremy gazed forlornly at the ceiling. His physical tension being redundant now, he let it go. After a moment he murmured, "What're you going to do?" It was an admission.

"Perhaps nothing," Alice said.

Too stunned to feel much of good or bad, Jeremy said, "Yes, dear."

"But I don't know yet. We shall have to see. It depends how you go on. After all, what you did was out of love for me."

"True," Jeremy said. "So true."

"And that has to be taken into consideration."

"Yes, dear."

"In any case, I don't see much point in you paying your debt to society in the usual way—spending years and years in prison. That wouldn't be serving, it would only be costing the state a lot of money."

"Terribly true. Terribly."

Alice said, "But of course you must pay in some way. Serve. Perhaps you can help the state and society by doing good. You could work with charities. You could become involved with community affairs. You could, in general, be more committed. We'll have to see."

"Yes," he said softly, deadly. He was beginning to feel again, at least to the extent of being amazed at how suddenly everything had changed. It had taken only a few minutes, a few words.

"We'll talk no more of it for the present," Alice said. "I need sleep."

"Yes, dear."

She made a movement, as though to get up. "First, though, I must have a glass of milk."

"Let me do it, darling," Jeremy said, sitting quickly. "I'll get it for you."

Alice renestled. "Oh, very well."

"And how about a little snack? You must be hungry. A snack, darling?"

"Well . . ."

"A nice sandwich and a couple of biscuits and a glass of milk," Jeremy coaxed. He thought he would set it out prettily on a tray, with a lace cloth, a mitred napkin, and a flower.

Alice said, "All right, Jeremy."

He rumpled fast out of bed, ignored robe and slippers, left the room, and went downstairs. "Don't go to sleep!" he called back lightly.

At the stairfoot he stopped.

Jeremy stopped and his eyes became dull. His face sagged like a lifted pancake. He put uncertain fingers to his lips. With horror he had suddenly seen, and was still seeing, how his future was going to be.

There they were before him now, stark and cruel visions of himself on streetcorners and sitting at card tables and ambling in picket lines and cleaning the house in mob-cap and apron and going to the store with a shopping basket and washing dishes and . . .

From the bedroom above came a vocal sound. It was Alice clearing her throat.

Jeremy hustled toward the kitchen.